# Rejoicing in Hope

by

# Frances Blok Popovich

A Missionary Novel
About 63,000 words

Sequel to *Never Forsaken* and *Unexpected Joy*

Published by Fidlar Doubleday

# Rejoicing in Hope

© 2009 Frances Blok Popovich

*Rejoicing in Hope*
By Frances Blok Popovich

Printed in the United States of America
ISBN 978-1-61623-229-0

All rights are reserved solely by the author. The author guarantees that all contents are original and do not infringe upon the legal rights of any other person or work. No part of this book may be reproduced in any form without the permission of the author. The views expressed in this book are not necessarily those of the publisher.

Unless otherwise indicated, Bible quotations are taken from the New International Version. Copyright © 1973, 1978 by the International Bible Society. Used by permission of Zondervan Bible Publishers, Grand Rapids, Michigan, 49506.

The author thanks Diane Bloem for editing this book, as well as the two previous books in this series, *Never Forsaken*, and *Unexpected Joy*.

Cover by Patricia Rasch

2500 Breton Woods Drive, SE
Suite 2051
Grand Rapids, Michigan 49512

Phone: 616-455-3809

E-mail: franpopovich6@aol.com

# Rejoicing in Hope

## Table of Contents

Copyright Page . . . . . . . . . . . . . . . . . . . . . . . . . . . . . . ii
Table of Contents . . . . . . . . . . . . . . . . . . . . . . . . . . . . iii
Prologue . . . . . . . . . . . . . . . . . . . . . . . . . . . . . . . . . . . . 1
Chapter 1 . . . . . . . . . . . . . . . . . . . . . . . . . . . . . . . . . . . 3
Chapter 2 . . . . . . . . . . . . . . . . . . . . . . . . . . . . . . . . . . 11
Chapter 3 . . . . . . . . . . . . . . . . . . . . . . . . . . . . . . . . . . 15
Chapter 4 . . . . . . . . . . . . . . . . . . . . . . . . . . . . . . . . . . 19
Chapter 5 . . . . . . . . . . . . . . . . . . . . . . . . . . . . . . . . . . 23
Chapter 6 . . . . . . . . . . . . . . . . . . . . . . . . . . . . . . . . . . 29
Chapter 7 . . . . . . . . . . . . . . . . . . . . . . . . . . . . . . . . . . 37
Chapter 8 . . . . . . . . . . . . . . . . . . . . . . . . . . . . . . . . . . 45
Chapter 9 . . . . . . . . . . . . . . . . . . . . . . . . . . . . . . . . . . 53
Chapter 10 . . . . . . . . . . . . . . . . . . . . . . . . . . . . . . . . . 59
Chapter 11 . . . . . . . . . . . . . . . . . . . . . . . . . . . . . . . . . 67
Chapter 12 . . . . . . . . . . . . . . . . . . . . . . . . . . . . . . . . . 75
Chapter 13 . . . . . . . . . . . . . . . . . . . . . . . . . . . . . . . . . 81
Chapter 14 . . . . . . . . . . . . . . . . . . . . . . . . . . . . . . . . . 87
Chapter 15 . . . . . . . . . . . . . . . . . . . . . . . . . . . . . . . . . 93
Chapter 16 . . . . . . . . . . . . . . . . . . . . . . . . . . . . . . . . . 99
Chapter 17 . . . . . . . . . . . . . . . . . . . . . . . . . . . . . . . . 107
Chapter 18 . . . . . . . . . . . . . . . . . . . . . . . . . . . . . . . . 113

# Rejoicing in Hope

Chapter 19 . . . . . . . . . . . . . . . . . . . . . . . . . . .119
Chapter 20 . . . . . . . . . . . . . . . . . . . . . . . . . . .125
Chapter 21 . . . . . . . . . . . . . . . . . . . . . . . . . . .133
Chapter 22 . . . . . . . . . . . . . . . . . . . . . . . . . . .139
Chapter 23 . . . . . . . . . . . . . . . . . . . . . . . . . . .147
Chapter 24 . . . . . . . . . . . . . . . . . . . . . . . . . . .153
Chapter 25 . . . . . . . . . . . . . . . . . . . . . . . . . . .161
Chapter 26 . . . . . . . . . . . . . . . . . . . . . . . . . . .169
Chapter 27 . . . . . . . . . . . . . . . . . . . . . . . . . . .177
Chapter 28 . . . . . . . . . . . . . . . . . . . . . . . . . . .185
Chapter 29 . . . . . . . . . . . . . . . . . . . . . . . . . . .193
Chapter 30 . . . . . . . . . . . . . . . . . . . . . . . . . . .199
Chapter 31 . . . . . . . . . . . . . . . . . . . . . . . . . . .207
Chapter 32 . . . . . . . . . . . . . . . . . . . . . . . . . . .215
Chapter 33 . . . . . . . . . . . . . . . . . . . . . . . . . . .223
Chapter 34 . . . . . . . . . . . . . . . . . . . . . . . . . . .231
Chapter 35 . . . . . . . . . . . . . . . . . . . . . . . . . . .239
Chapter 36 . . . . . . . . . . . . . . . . . . . . . . . . . . .245
Chapter 37 . . . . . . . . . . . . . . . . . . . . . . . . . . .255

# Prologue

Cecily Spears sat on her bed, studying the portrait she held in her hands. The picture was a glamour pose of Ingrid White—Cecily's mother—taken when she graduated from high school. She married Randall (Randy) Spears before she was twenty and gave birth to Cecily and Randy Junior. Ingrid soon became restless and bored. She began to pursue a promiscuous lifestyle, and took up the recreational use of drugs. Her husband—the children's father—sued for divorce when Cecily was five years old and her little brother, Randy Junior, was two. The court gave the parents joint custody, and the children continued to live with their mother.

When Randy became aware that his ex-wife was neglecting their children, he took them to his mother's home in Texarkana and old Mrs. Spears had taken over their care. Randy subsequently sued for and obtained sole legal custody of his children. His ex-wife's mother (Linda White) had contested the suit, but the court decided in the father's favor. It proved to be providential, because his ex-mother-in-law died of cancer two years later. When he married Susan he debated taking over the care of the children himself, but both Susan and his mother advised against it. The children preferred to stay with their grandmother, and so it was decided.

Memories of her mother had become hazy with time, but Cecily still cherished the remembrance of her mother's warm hugs and encouraging smiles. Even the fact that her mother often left Cecily and her little brother alone all night to pursue men and the drugs she craved, could not entirely obliterate Cecily's warm memories of her mother.

After they had been moved to their grandmother's home, the children saw little of their mother. Old Mrs. Spears had insisted on supervising any contact Ingrid had with her

## Rejoicing in Hope

children, and Ingrid resented the intrusion. Several years later she married an older man and moved to Tucson, Arizona.

Cecily was thirteen years old and Randy Junior was ten when Ingrid's sister Mary visited the Spears family to inform the children of their mother's death from a drug overdose. They had never met their aunt before, who had spent nearly ten years in Brazil as a missionary-translator,[1] but she brought them news that she explained was encouraging. She told them that their mother had smiled and whispered Jesus' name as she died. Though she had lived badly, their aunt insisted, she had died well.[2]

Shortly thereafter Mary White married Jason Nealey and she settled in Cedar Hill, Texas, where Jason lived in a large home he had inherited from his parents. During the years they occasionally visited with the Spears children, but Cecily knew almost nothing about her aunt's life during the years when she had worked in Brazil.

The years and the cares had taken their toll on old Mrs. Spears' health, and when she began to show signs of dementia, she was moved to the Radcliffe Manor's memory unit, and the children—now in their early and mid teens—were moved to their father's home.

Cecily had never felt comfortable with her stepmother, and moved into a dormitory when she started college. Randy Junior got along better with Susan, but confided to his sister that he planned to move out after his graduation from high school in June.

---

[1] Read *Never Forsaken*
[2] Read *Unexpected Joy*

# Rejoicing in Hope

## Chapter 1

"Cecily!"

Someone rattled the knob at the locked door of Cecily's bedroom. Cecily sighed, put down the eight-by-ten portrait of her own mother, and moved to unlock the door.

"Come in."

The door opened and her stepmother, Susan Spears entered.

"Are you ready to go? Your dad is waiting in the garage for you."

Cecily smothered an impatient rejoinder. "Tell him I'll be there in a minute." She picked up the portrait of her mother and carefully put it back into its carton.

Susan frowned, but said nothing. *How can she be moping over her mother, when all that woman did was run after men and drugs? She even died from an overdose."* She stood at the door, waiting for Cecily to obey the summons.

Seeing that her stepmother was impatiently waiting for her to leave, Cecily grabbed her purse and a sweater and left the room, waiting at the door for her stepmother to step outside, and then locked the door behind her.

Her father had backed the car out of the garage, and as Cecily joined him, he reached over and opened the passenger door for her. "We need to hurry, because we want to visit your grandma before she has her lunch."

Cecily nodded and fastened her seatbelt.

"Have you heard from your Aunt Mary lately?" Her father's question broke into Cecily's thoughts. Mary Nealey was the sister of his children's mother, Ingrid.

## Rejoicing in Hope

"She phoned Sunday and invited me to stay with her this summer."

Randy raised his eyebrows. "Are you planning to do that?"

Cecily shrugged her shoulders. "I'd like to," she admitted. "But I need to find a job, to pay for my tuition next year." Tuitions had risen astronomically during the past decade, and a job was now essential.

"Maybe your Aunt Mary can help you there," he suggested.

Cecily nodded. "I did mention it, and she said she would look into it for me."

Her father made no response and the silence continued until they arrived at the Radcliffe Manor.

Cecily was twenty years old, with thick, wavy brown hair and long dark eyelashes over beautiful, large, luminous gray eyes that looked seriously out on the world. Her looks were striking, but her reserve discouraged easy intimacy with strangers. She was a junior in college, a good student, but, being quiet and shy, she did not project herself among her classmates. She tended to hold back, but once she realized that the person could be trusted, she was a faithful friend.

*****

In the corridors of the memory unit old Mrs. Spears was pacing the hall, as usual. Driven by an inner restlessness, she seemed unable to sit still. Her son greeted her affectionately with a hug and kiss. Then Cecily put her arms around her grandmother, and said, "Glad to see you, Grandma. How are you?"

Old Mrs. Spears blinked up at Cecily. She had apparently forgotten or mislaid her glasses. Then she smiled.

# Rejoicing in Hope

"I'm so glad to see you, Hilda. I've really missed you."

"But I'm not Hilda, Grandma; I'm your granddaughter, Randy's girl. I'm Cecily."

Randy interrupted: "She isn't Hilda, Mom. Hilda died years ago in an automobile accident."

Mrs. Spears seemed not to have heard either of them, and continued, "I've been looking everywhere for you, Hilda, but all the doors are locked, and they won't let me out."

Randy broke in, "Let's sit down somewhere, Mom. You look worn out."

"I'm exhausted, but I wanted to find Hilda. I'm so glad she came."

Randy led them to an alcove and coaxed his mother to sit down in one of the easy chairs. Mrs. Spears leaned back wearily. She reached her hand out to her granddaughter, and repeated, "I'm so glad to see you again, Hilda."

Cecily grasped her grandmother's hand and responded tenderly, "I'm very glad to be here, Grandma."

On the return home, both Randy and his daughter were quiet. Cecily glanced at her father's profile as he drove, and thought, *Grandma seems like a different person. She must be as lonely inside now as I used to be when she took us into her home. I wish I could comfort her as she did me, years ago!*

*****

That evening Cecily received a phone call from her Aunt Mary Nealey in Cedar Hill. To her delight, her aunt called to tell her of a choice of jobs awaiting her pleasure once the college semester was ended.

# Rejoicing in Hope

"Cecily, we found three job openings for you here in Cedar Hill. The first one is in the office of your Uncle Jason's shipping company. His current secretary is getting married next month and will go to the mission field with her new husband. The second opening is as a nanny for one of our friends' children, and the third is as a sales associate in a large discount store. They are all willing to hold the summer position for you, and there is only one drawback. They need to know if you are not interested in the jobs they are offering. Because if you aren't, they would like to offer them to someone else on or before May first."

"That's great, only I don't know which one I prefer. What do they pay?"

"They all pay about the same: the wages of temporary summer help. Would you be free to come down here sometime later this month and interview them?"

"I think I can come down to Cedar Hill the end of this week. Would I be able to interview them on a Friday or Saturday?" Cecily pulled the pocket agenda out of her purse and studied April's schedule.

"I think that would be fine. Why don't you plan to stay with us this weekend? We haven't seen much of you lately." Cecily could hear the smile in her aunt's voice.

"Thanks, Aunt Mary. I'd like that."

*****

On the Thursday before Easter, known as Maundy Thursday, Cecily was driving down to Dallas from Texarkana on Interstate 30 in her little Prizm car. She was full of anticipation for the weekend. She had tried to coax her brother Randy to drive down to Cedar Hill with her, but Randy—now a senior in high school—had other plans for the weekend. So she took off on the three hour trip on her own.

# Rejoicing in Hope

As she drove, Cecily recalled the first time she had met her Aunt Mary. That was seven years ago, before her aunt had married Uncle Jason, and her name was still White. She had come to Texarkana to bring the sad new of their mother Ingrid's death to her niece and nephew. She told how Ingrid had died smiling, apparently seeing Jesus in her final moments as she spoke his name. Cecily remembered how her Aunt Mary had emphasized that, although she had lived badly, her mother had died well. *I want to ask her about that. I've never forgotten it. What does it all mean?*

After Aunt Mary returned to Cedar Hill, Cecily had begged her grandmother to take them to church. The Spears family was not religious, but to humor them, Marcia Spears agreed to take the children to a nearby church. Cecily had gone to a class for adolescents, but the class seemed to be only interested in dances sponsored by the church. When the teacher gave the teenagers an opportunity for questions, she finally ventured to raise her hand. She asked, "Where do people go when they die?"

A painful silence had fallen upon the group. They had all stared at her. Just as Cecily was wishing that the ground would swallow her up, her teacher told her that she was too young to be thinking about death. It was the last time Cecily had been brave enough to ask anyone about death, but it was not the last time she wondered about it. She had refused to attend the church the following Sunday, and her grandmother seemed relieved to cancel their attendance.

Aunt Mary and Uncle Jason had visited them a few times over the years, but Cecily had never had a chance to talk to her Aunt Mary alone. Surely this weekend or even later, during the summer, she would have a chance to talk to Aunt Mary about her mother's death.

*****

## Rejoicing in Hope

With a sigh of relief Cecily pulled up onto the Nealey driveway. She had worried about getting lost in an unknown neighborhood, but her Aunt Mary had given very clear directions and she arrived without a problem.

As she got out of the car, her aunt came out of the house to greet her. Behind her, little five-year-old Jay slipped out of the door. He shyly hid behind his mother's skirts.

"Hi there, Jay! How are you?" Cecily greeted her little cousin.

Mary offered to help carry Cecily's baggage into the house, and Cecily pointed out the cartons that contained her baggage for the weekend. The other cartons were going on to her college dorm after the weekend and could stay packed in the trunk.

Mary led Cecily into the house and helped her carry the cartons to an upstairs bedroom. Then she led her downstairs to the kitchen, where they sat down to have a cup of coffee. The aroma of the coffee gave the kitchen a homey feeling.

Cecily studied her Aunt Mary, and decided that while she had aged a little bit, she hadn't changed very much. She was just below average in height, and had a stocky build. Her hair was attractively styled and waved and her smile was warm and inviting. She lacked her late sister's beauty, but Cecily felt drawn to her.

"You look just like I remember you, Aunt Mary."

Mary laughed. "I guess people of my age don't change much until they get to their sixties, and then they start to show their age.

Cecily looked around. "Where is Uncle Jason? Isn't he here?"

"Your Uncle Jason's at work. Thursdays are busy workdays for him. We can go and join him for lunch and

## Rejoicing in Hope

then you can interview him. Meanwhile, we can visit the discount store's personnel manager first."

"What about the lady who needs a nanny? When do I see her?"

"We'll call on her at 4 PM. If we can't get to see her today, we'll try to see her tomorrow."

"I have to drive back to the dorm early Sunday afternoon, Aunt Mary. I don't want to drive alone at night."

"I don't think we'll have any trouble getting to meet her. She'll be at our class Sunday morning. She's a member of our Pilgrim Sunday school class, too."

*****

As they enjoyed their lunch, Mary confided: "I just got some wonderful news. My former partner from Brazil is coming to Dallas with her family for a translation seminar. They have three children, and will be staying with us."

"Is she a Brazilian, Aunt Mary?"

Mary laughed. "No, she's from Michigan, but we worked together in the Guará tribe in Brazil. That's quite a long time ago now. She's a wonderful person, and I know you'll love her."

Cecily's eyes widened. "What did you do in Brazil, Aunt Mary?"

"We learned and analyzed the Guará Indian language. Then we translated Bible stories for them."

"Why would you do that? What was that like?"

Mary looked thoughtfully at her niece.

"We went there to teach them about God and his love for them. Since they only spoke their own language, we had

# Rejoicing in Hope

to learn it in order to tell them about God. We taught them to read and we translated stories from the Bible for them."

*Why did they bother? Why would Indians need to know about God?* She opened her mouth to ask, when the telephone rang. After her Aunt Mary hung up the phone, Cecily thought better of asking that question. *It sounds like such a dumb question. Maybe I can find out this summer.*

*****

Cecily helped her Aunt Mary with preparations for supper. The kitchen was old fashioned, but the appliances were modern. Cecily carefully laid out the china, silverware and napkins on the large dining room table. While she did this, she mulled over the questions that were clamoring to be asked. The question that had shocked the Sunday school class into silence still needed to be asked. When could she ask it? She was working up courage to frame her question, when little Jay stumbled into the kitchen, crying and holding a skinned knee. Aunt Mary was busy mashing potatoes, so Cecily picked the little boy up and carried him to the bathroom to bathe his wound. Then she applied a Band-Aid, which seemed to comfort him a great deal. He smiled through his tears at her, and she smiled back.

Mary noticed the mutual appreciation, and silently thanked the Lord.

# Rejoicing in Hope

## Chapter 2

Mary had warned her niece that the family would be attending church on Easter Sunday morning. "We'll go to the sunrise service, have a continental breakfast at the church, and afterwards attend Sunday school. I hope you'll come with us, Cecily. We'd love to have you."

Cecily had a flashback of the embarrassing Sunday school class of years ago.

"Sure, I'd be glad to go. Could I go to your class with you, rather than to a kids' class?"

"We have a college age class and a singles' class, if you would like to go to either one. But you may certainly attend the Pilgrim's Class with your Uncle Jason and me, if you'd rather."

"I think I would, if you please." So Cecily had attended the couples' class with the post-college adults.

The Sunday school lesson was about heaven, building on that morning's celebration of Christ's resurrection. Cecily listened with rapt attention. When the teacher offered an opportunity to ask questions, Cecily decided to risk it:

"Where do people go when they die?"

The class fell silent, but it was not the silence of embarrassment, but of respect for a solemn question.

The teacher smiled to encourage her.

"That is one of the most important questions we can ever ask. When God created mankind, he created them with the ability to relate to him. When mankind sinned, we lost that affinity, and became estranged from him. But God loves

## Rejoicing in Hope

us so much that he sent his only son to die, to pay our sin-debt so that God could again accept us as friends. When we trust in Jesus who died to reconcile us to God, God accepts us as his children. When God's children die, they go to heaven to be with God and to enjoy him forever.[1] That's what Easter is all about."

Cecily decided to risk another question: "What happens to people who don't "reconcile" with God. Where do they go when they die?"

"The Bible says that all of us are condemned to live and die estranged from God, unless we accept what Jesus has done to pay the sin-debt for us. When we reject Jesus Christ we remain estranged from God forever. That's what hell is: it's the eternal punishment of God's enemies. It's being lost forever in darkest space."[2]

The words sunk deeply into Cecily's soul. Her eyes sought those of her Aunt Mary, and she saw the tears glistening there.

It was a very quiet Cecily at the Sunday dinner table. After she helped her Aunt to clear the table and put away the leftovers, she decided to pack up and leave for the dorm. Mary gently asked to talk with her a few minutes before she left.

Jason washed the dishes—his Sunday chore—while Mary followed Cecily to her room.

"Do you still have your Bible?" She had given Cecily and her brother Randy Bibles several years before.

"Yes, but I don't understand it. It's hard to make sense out of it."

---

[1] Jude 24, 25
[2] Jude 13

# Rejoicing in Hope

"Let's kneel together and ask God to teach you what you need to learn from the Bible. He wants you to understand it, because the Bible is God's love letter to us."

Cecily knelt and began to cry. Mary knelt beside her, put her arm around her, and prayed for her. Then she urged Cecily to pray, to ask God to accept her, to teach her, and to make her his child. Stammering, Cecily obeyed. Then both stood up. Cecily threw her arms around her aunt's neck, and said, "I really want to be God's child."

"God is reaching out to you and he invites you to give your heart to him.[1] I'll be praying for you every day."

Mary accompanied Cecily to her car, and saw her off.

Jason came out of the kitchen and said, "That little one was longing to give her heart to God. It showed all over."

*****

As Cecily drove northward, her thoughts were tumultuous. She sensed an overwhelming desire to pray. This frightened her a little. *What should I say to God? I don't even know how to pray.* She felt a lump in her throat and an urge to cry took hold of her. She pulled over to the shoulder of the highway, bowed her head over the steering wheel, and gave way to the emotion that threatened to overwhelm her.

"God, I want so much to talk to you, to ask you to take over my life and make something worthwhile out of it. Thank you for loving me, for forgiving my sins and selfishness. Please, please show me how I can love you and live the way you want me to."

Cecily gave way to her emotions and sobbed out her prayer to God. She was so absorbed in her prayer, that she was unaware when a motorcycle policeman pulled up on the

---

[1] Proverbs 3:5-8, 23:26

## Rejoicing in Hope

shoulder of the highway directly in front of her car. She was startled to hear a knock on the driver's window. After a moment's hesitation, she rolled down her window several inches, and wiped the tears from her eyes with the back of her hand.

"Is something wrong, Miss?"

Cecily was confused, uncertain how to answer him.

"I'm fine. I just stopped because I...." She was uncertain how she could explain why she had pulled off the highway.

"Yes?" The officer noticed the tear-stained face. "Have you taken any drugs, Miss?" He checked her for signs of intoxication or addiction.

"No, I just pulled over because I felt like..." She could not think of any explanation that would be convincing. She couldn't tell him she stopped because she wanted to pray, could she? She gave up the attempt to explain, and asked, "May I go now?"

"Yes, if you're sure you're all right. Would you like your parents to come and pick you up?"

"No, thanks. I'm on the way back to my college dorm now. This was my spring break and I spent this weekend with my uncle and aunt."

The officer stood back, and waited while she rolled up the window, started up the car, and pulled back onto the highway. Cecily drove away, with a sense of relief that gradually turned into an amazing joy bubbling inside. The heavy feelings were gone, and she felt sure that God loved her.

# Rejoicing in Hope

## Chapter 3

During the final two months of her junior year at the college, Cecily worked several changes into her life. She looked up the student representative of the Intervarsity Christian Fellowship and began to attend their meetings. As she made new friends in the fellowship, she gradually stopped attending some of the parties where drinking was a prominent feature. Although drinking parties had never attracted her, she usually stood around with a cocktail in her hand in order to blend in with the crowd. She endured some teasing from her friends as she began to spend more time reading her Bible and attending the Bible studies, but they mostly left her alone. Some of her new friends invited her to attend church with them on Sundays, and she joined a pre-membership class to learn the basics of the Christian Faith.

Cecily came home for a weekend in early May and her family noticed a change in her. Susan found it hard to define, but Cecily was more relaxed and readily volunteered to help her stepmother with the domestic chores. Susan eyed her with misgiving, feeling uneasy about these changes, unable to understand her. She had some grounds to be uneasy, because one of her friends, Dora Evans, had a son who regularly dated Cecily, but who was troubled at the changes in her.

While most of her college friends paid scant attention to Cecily's recent absorption in Bible studies, Don tried to convince her to drop her new friends and return to the old partying cycle. He said, "Are you crazy or what? Why have you gone on this religious kick? You're no fun anymore."

Cecily was taken aback.

# Rejoicing in Hope

"What do you mean? I think I'm a lot happier than I was a few months ago. I never did enjoy those drinking parties, so they're no loss to me. Why does it upset you that I don't go to parties that I never enjoyed, anyway?"

"It's not that," Don sputtered. "It's the religious kick you're on. Reading the Bible and praying." He emphasized the words "Bible" and "praying" as if they were disgusting activities.

"Have you ever tried either of those two things yourself? Why run them down when you've never tried them?"

Because of Don's complaint Cecily was not surprised when her stepmother took her to task for embarking on her new "religious whims." "Where did you get your new religious ideas, Cecily? Are you thinking of joining one of these sects and abandoning the world or something like that? I suppose you got those ideas from your Aunt Mary."

Susan Spears said this in front of her husband, fully expecting his support in discouraging Cecily's new friendships and activities. To her surprise, Randy intervened.

"Just leave her alone, Susan. Her new friends won't do her any harm. She could do much worse than attend some Bible studies."

"But...," Susan sputtered. Randy shrugged his shoulders and changed the subject to ask Cecily what job she had chosen for the summer. Cecily replied that she had chosen to work in her uncle's office at the shipping company.

"That's a good idea. It will give you some good experience to put into your job résumé after you graduate."

Later, Cecily joined her father in the den. He was watching the news on television, and glanced up at his daughter.

"Something on your mind, Cecily?"

# Rejoicing in Hope

"Well, yes...I was wondering about alcoholism. Is it sure that the tendency is inherited?"

Randy Spears turned off the television, and looked thoughtfully at his daughter. *Is it fear of becoming an alcoholic that drives my daughter to affiliate with this conservative Christian group on campus?*

"Have you done any internet research on that topic, Cecily?"

"Yes, actually I have. Most say that there may be an element of heredity in alcoholism, but it still seems debatable. There are several other factors that contribute to it, such as a personality problem, social influences, insecurity, and of course, habit."

Her father nodded. "You have two parents. I never had a drinking problem. There is no reason to assume that you have inherited your mother's weakness in this area, is there?"

"No, not really. That is, I never took more than a sip or two at our parties, but it seems that one of the characteristics of an alcoholic is denial that they have a drinking problem."

"True. I must admit that I've been relieved to notice that you haven't taken to party drinking. I think you've taken the most important step to prevent the disease. You try to avoid drinking whenever you can, which is very wise."

"You don't drink, Daddy—or I should say, you don't drink much. I don't remember ever seeing you drink at home. You only seem to drink a little in parties. I've tried to imitate you, Daddy, as the way I would like to be."

Randy smiled at the implied compliment. "I used to drink more. In fact, I think your mother started to be a problem drinker after we were married. When I saw what it did to her, I stopped drinking myself."

# Rejoicing in Hope

"The kids I go around with now don't drink at all. They think it's something a Christian shouldn't do. Just like smoking. They think it's a sin."

"I don't know if I would go that far, but I certainly think that you're better off if you don't smoke or drink."

*****

As the semester wore on, Cecily saw little of Don Evans, although he still accompanied her to a few campus activities. She ran into him in the cafeteria and hallways several times during the final weeks, and noticed he was often engrossed in conversation with the same pretty blond girl. While she felt a bit uncomfortable about it, she had to admit that she was far from being heartbroken over it. In turn, she began to respond more to the advances of the boys in her Christian group.

In May Cecily took her final exams and prepared to move out of the dorm and into her Aunt Mary's home in Cedar Hill. She looked forward to working in her Uncle Jason's office for the summer. From telephone conversations with her Aunt Mary she learned that the Kruyters (Aunt Mary's friends from Brazil) would be coming to stay with them during the month of June to participate in the translation seminar that would be held in Dallas. Privately Cecily wondered what kind of people these foreign missionaries would be, but she did not voice her doubts.

# Rejoicing in Hope

## Chapter 4

On the first Sunday that Cecily spent in Cedar Hill she joined the college-age Sunday school class. As her uncle Jason introduced her to the class teacher, he also introduced one of the members, Paula Ballard, who smiled warmly at her, and said, "We've prayed for you for at least seven years. Oh, not every day, but often. You're Mary's family, and she's special."

Cecily stared. "Why were you praying for me?"

"Mostly because you're special to Mary, and she's special to us."

"Thank you." Cecily was not sure whether she liked being prayed for. *What does that mean?* Cecily looked at Paula's friendly smile, and decided that she meant it as a gesture of encouragement. She relaxed and returned the smile. Paula led her to seats near the front of the classroom.

After the class Paula led her to where her family was waiting. Paula's parents—Mike and Jean Ballard—were in the lobby with Paula's sister Carol and her fiancé. After Paula finished introducing everyone, her brother Gary joined the family group. Jason and Mary Nealey were the last to come, and they were leading young Jay by the hand.

Cecily wondered why they were all standing in the lobby and waiting. *Waiting for what or for whom?* Obviously the Ballards were close friends of the Nealeys. Paula noticed her bewilderment, and explained:

"We usually eat together after the service and discuss the interesting parts of the sermon or of the Sunday school lesson. It makes our Sundays more special." Turning to her

## Rejoicing in Hope

brother Gary, she asked, "Where is your girlfriend? Isn't she joining us for dinner?"

Gary shrugged his shoulders.

"I guess not." He did not explain, and after a moment of silence, no one asked him for any explanation.

Jean Ballard looked concerned, but hastily suggested they leave for the Ballard house where they would eat their Sunday dinner. Mary explained in an aside to Cecily:

"We lead such busy lives that we like to take this little break in our week and talk about some of our current joys and problems. We usually have a potluck dinner together."

Cecily stole a look at Gary Ballard. He was one of the handsomest men she had ever met. He was older, probably somewhere in his late twenties. He noticed her interest, so she averted her eyes and joined her uncle and aunt in the church parking lot.

The Nealeys stopped at their home—before heading for the Ballard home—to pick up the dishes of food Mary had prepared for the potluck.

The large Ballard dining room table seated six comfortably, but left two persons unaccommodated. Jean Ballard brought out a sturdy card table, and invited the engaged couple to sit at it. They all took their places at the tables, the men holding the chairs for the women. Cecily was privately impressed. Most of her friends did not observe these small courtesies.

After they had settled themselves at the small table, Cecily leaned over and asked, "When are you planning to be married?"

Carol smiled. "We plan to marry in August."

# Rejoicing in Hope

While Carol and Jacob explained the details of their wedding plans, Gary was searching his memories for details of Cecily's background. *I wasn't paying a lot of attention when Mary told us about Cecily's mother, but I seem to remember that she had abandoned her family and was heavily into various addictions. Mary went to Tucson twice to be with Cecily's mother, as I remember. The last time her mother took an overdose of drugs and died. Cecily doesn't seem like anyone who is into drugs and stuff like that at all. I'd like to ask Mary about her some time.*

Cecily was absorbed in Carol's wedding plans and was consequently unaware of Gary's interest. Paula was playing with little Jay, with whom she seemed to be on the best terms. When the meal was over, everyone rinsed off their dishes and stacked them in the dishwasher. The young people filed down to the basement recreation room to play pool and ping pong. Jason and Mary took their young son home to nap, because he was becoming cross and whiny. Gary promised to take Cecily home later.

On the drive to the Nealey home Cecily asked Gary about his work as a civil engineer. She didn't want to show her ignorance about his profession, so she merely asked whether he enjoyed his work.

"Actually, it's what I always wanted to do. I work with my Dad, and it's been satisfying. Lately, however, I've been wondering if there isn't more to life than planning cities."

"What else would you like to do?" Cecily was puzzled.

"If I knew that, I'd work at getting into it. It's only a feeling I have that I should do something that would bring eternal rewards. Does that make sense to you?" Gary turned to look at her.

"It makes a lot of sense. I've been praying and asking God to make my life worthwhile. I have no idea what kind of

# Rejoicing in Hope

work that would be, but it probably would be something that wouldn't earn me much by way of salary."

"Exactly! I bring home a big salary, and my girlfriend thinks I should be satisfied with that. She thinks I should 'stop dreaming' and settle down in the 'real world.'"

At this point Gary entered the Nealey driveway, and Cecily unlatched her safety belt and prepared to leave the car. She turned to Gary:

"Have you thought that maybe God is calling you to do something special that won't bring in much of a salary? Maybe something that will bring you lasting satisfaction?"

Gary looked at her with new respect.

"Yes, that's what I've been thinking."

Cecily thanked him for bringing her home and let herself out of the car. As she was leaving she lingered to say, "Don't give up on your dream. Ask God to show you what it is he wants you to do." As she turned to enter the back door of the Nealey home, she reflected that she, a new believer, had a lot of nerve giving advice to a longtime believer like Gary.

# Rejoicing in Hope

## Chapter 5

Cecily knew that she had never been as happy as she was that summer. The Ballards were intimate friends of the Nealeys and considered themselves family. Cecily became familiar with Paula Ballard who was a sophomore in college and only a year younger than Cecily. At first Cecily judged Paula to be much younger than she, however both girls were shy and that forged a common bond between them. Carol was several years older and was wrapped up in her romantic plans and in her fiancé Jacob. Jacob was very approachable and Cecily thought he fit nicely into the Ballard family. She wasn't precisely sure how she felt about Gary, but knew that she admired him more than anyone else. She met Gary's girlfriend several times that summer, but never really got to know her. She was a beautiful girl and seemed to be outgoing, but she did not warm up to Gary's family. She was supposedly a Christian girl, but Cecily thought she was brittle rather than spiritual.

Just about the time that Cecily had settled comfortably into the Nealey family, Mary began to prepare for the month-long visit of the Kruyter family. Rachel Kruyter had been Mary's partner when they were single and worked among the Guará Indians. After a year they separated and took other assignments.[1] Rachel (formerly Dykstra) met and married Richard Kruyter and they formed a translation team to work among the Guará Indians. Mary, on the other hand, met her former classmate Jason Nealey while she was on furlough teaching literacy principles to missionary candidates.[2] They

---

[1] Read *Never Forsaken*
[2] Read *Unexpected Joy*

## Rejoicing in Hope

fell in love and were married. Mary was granted the status of "home assigned" and still taught literacy principles in the Linguistics Institute twice a year.

*****

The Kruyter family arrived in Texas from Michigan the end of May. They had left tropical Brazil two weeks earlier just as the weather turned cooler in the southern hemisphere. They spent a week with the Kruyter relatives in Iowa, and enjoyed the wonder of a northern hemisphere spring, when all of nature seems reborn. They spent another week with the Dykstra families in Grand Rapids. Then they flew down to Dallas-Fort Worth and were greeted with great joy by the Nealey family.

Cecily drove to the airport with her Aunt Mary and little Jay to receive them. The flight was on time, and they waited for them at the baggage carousels. Cecily watched as a family of five entered the room to collect their baggage. A tall slim man, who Cecily assumed was Richard, carried a little boy while a tall slender young woman carried a baby. A little blond girl clung to her mother's hand and looked warily about her.

Mary rushed to greet her friends, while Cecily followed more slowly with little Jay, who was carrying a red plastic toy truck in one hand. She waited as Mary embraced her friend Rachel and then turned to introduce Cecily to the family. The little girl was six-year-old Laura Marie, the three-year-old was Jerry, and the baby in Rachel's arms was Hannah.

Little Jay Nealey, five years old, held back, and measured little Jerry. Then he thrust the toy truck he was carrying into Jerry's hands. That broke the ice, and Jerry smiled. The little boys got down on their hands and knees in the baggage room to play with the truck.

# Rejoicing in Hope

Although little Jay was only five years old, he was a quiet, contented child, and the Nealey house was usually hushed. Now with the coming of three other young children, one of them a baby, that changed. The house became a place of hustle and bustle. Cecily had never lived in a house with four young children, and was not sure that she would enjoy the experience. Rachel Kruyter seemed to be always busy with one or more of the children and she seemed to be washing clothes or bathing babies most of the time.

Mary explained to Cecily that Laura Marie was her *xará*, the Portuguese word for "namesake."

"The first part of her name is in honor of her maternal grandmother, and the second part (Marie) is for Mary, that's me. Little Jerry is named after Rachel's father who left the family when she was only seven, and the baby Hannah is named for Richard's mother who died of cancer when he was a teenager."

Cecily wondered where the custom of naming babies after family members had originated. *I wonder if my parents named me after someone. I never thought to ask how they chose my name.*

*****

After a few days the Kruyter children settled down into a routine. The translation seminar was scheduled to begin the following week, and then the three Kruyter children would go to the childcare during the mornings, leaving their mother free to attend the morning sessions. Cooking for nine rather than four kept Mary busy, and she reflected wryly that having the Kruyter children in the nursery during the mornings would help her get organized again. Cecily pitched in to relieve her of as much as she could before and after work.

# Rejoicing in Hope

Suppers were leisurely affairs that month. Rachel usually fed the two younger children first and put them to bed before Richard, Jason, and Cecily came home from work. Little Jay and Laura ate with the family and then were excused to the playroom, while the adults ate and conversed in the dining room.

Richard and Rachel had all kinds of interesting stories about their work and life with the Guará Indians to tell at the supper table. Richard told of a time when a small group of intoxicated Indians came to their hut, shouting what appeared to be threats and waving bows and arrows. He had only been there a few weeks and knew very little of the language. He wanted to keep the men out of the hut because he feared they were bent on some kind of violence, so he told Rachel to stay out of sight, and he slipped out the front door and greeted the men pleasantly. Apparently his genial manner confused them, and they gradually calmed down. He could not understand whatever they were trying to say, so they withdrew after a time, leaving Richard to rejoin Rachel inside the hut. Together they thanked God for his protection. Rachel had been praying inside the hut during the entire episode.

Cecily looked shocked. "Weren't you scared to death?"

Richard's smile was rueful. "Rather. But I didn't know what else to do."

*****

Another evening Rachel told of an experience while translating First Thessalonians. A.J., the co-translator, was apparently deeply moved by the exhortations to holy living. He straightened up with a jerk, however, when Rachel introduced her preliminary translation of the fourth chapter of that epistle. Rachel had spent hours preparing the passage that dealt with Jesus Christ's second coming. Noticing that

# Rejoicing in Hope

A.J. had snapped to attention, she continued to read her Guará rendering of the passage at a slower, clearly articulated rate. When she finished reading the passage, A.J. broke in:

"Is Jesus coming back? Will he come here?" He indicated the rocky hills and green valleys that surrounded them.

Rachel caught herself just in time. She had been about to say, "No, not here. He'll be coming to Israel," when she realized that it was not the best answer. *Lord, what should I say? What would be the best answer?* Another verse flashed into her mind:

> *Look, he is coming with the clouds,*
> *And every eye will see him,*
> *Even those who pierced him;*
> *And all the peoples of the earth will mourn*
> *because of him. So shall it be! Amen.*[1]

She answered A.J., "In God's paper we read that everyone will see him when he comes."

A.J. heaved a sigh of relief. He said, "I knew it! Jesus is coming right here to the Guará reservation!"

---

[1] Revelation 1:7

# Rejoicing in Hope

# Rejoicing in Hope

## Chapter 6

One evening Jason introduced a topic for the family discussion.

"Mike Ballard stopped by the office today and we had a cup of coffee together. I don't think he has ever stopped to see me at work before in all the years we've been friends. I waited for him to tell me why he had come, because I didn't want to ask.

"Trying to help him say what was on his mind, I asked how the family was getting along. He said, 'Fine, healthwise. It's Gary who knocked the props from under me.'

"I waited for an explanation. Gary has always been a good boy, got top grades in school and was never in trouble. I know they've been worrying about the girl he's dating. They don't think she's right for him, but beyond that, I didn't know that they had any cause to worry."

Jason paused. Cecily tensed up. *What's wrong with Gary? Why are they worried about him?*

Jason continued.

"Gary has been working with his dad as a civil engineer. Mike brags that Gary is a natural. He does top work and gets along with all the guys. Now Mike says that Gary wants to get into missionary work in some foreign country. With all that money spent on his education, now he wants to throw it all over and go overseas.

"I asked Mike if Gary had talked to his fiancée about it, and Mike said he had. I waited for him to explain, but after a bit he just said that the girl told Gary that if he was going to

## Rejoicing in Hope

the mission field he would have to go alone. She was not about to make an idiot of herself to go with him."

Jason paused. "I asked Mike whether that had settled it for Gary, but he said no. Gary said he told her that God was first in his life, and God was calling him to go. As far as he was concerned, that settled it."

"Then what did she do?" Cecily couldn't hold back the questions. "Is he still determined to go?"

"He said that she gave him back his ring and told him that if he ever changed his mind, he could let her know. Then she left."

"How could she? Isn't she a Christian too?" Cecily was indignant. "What more could she want than a man who puts God first in his life?"

"Well, Mike and Jean are worried about his decision, because he's giving up his job security and they're sure he'll regret it in a few years. A missionary's salary is small enough when he goes with a reputable organization, but an itinerant or faith missionary has no guaranteed salary at all. What girl with any ambition will be willing to link her life to his?"

Richard Kruyter broke into the conversation.

"In a sense, that's what I did. I got a doctoral degree in order to be a seminary professor and I gladly gave up the respectable salary to become a Bible translator and live on freewill offerings."

Jason was taken aback.

"Do you mean that you have a doctor's degree and you still don't have a guaranteed salary?"

"The Bible Translation organization is called a "faith mission" for that very reason. None of us earns a guaranteed

# Rejoicing in Hope

salary, not even our administrators and the international heads of the mission."

Rachel interrupted to say, "We're required to meet a certain income quota that must be pledged before we may go to the field. Our supporting churches and friends pledge a certain amount per month or per year. How much we receive in terms of donations has nothing to do with the quality of our work."

Jason found this hard to believe. "Don't the administrators and CEOs get a higher quota than the field workers?"

Mary broke into the discussion. "Our quotas are based on family size and ministry needs, not on positions filled by the members. Someone who has generous friends and who communicates well usually receives more donations than someone who doesn't. But we do have what we call an 'undesignated fund' to help our members in case of a financial crisis. And that's not all. Some members routinely give to one colleague or another who has had a shortfall."

Jason was stunned. Mary looked at him with amazement. *Surely he must know all about that. He must know that I had no guaranteed salary when I was out on the field. When I married Jason I declined mission funds because my husband can support me very well. Apparently he never really understood.*

Jason rubbed his chin thoughtfully.

"Maybe we can bring this up next Sunday when we have a potluck dinner with the Ballards. That may help them to accept Gary's decision with less misgiving."

"Different mission organizations have different financial policies. It would be helpful to know what kind of work Gary wants to do, and research the mission organizations that specialize in that work, and then review their financial policies." Richard tried to be helpful. He looked around the group sitting at the table, and wondered which of them would have time to do research on faith missions before Sunday.

Cecily volunteered shyly, "I'll do some Internet research. That would be the fastest way to get information on that topic."

Jason sighed in relief. "Great! I know that Mike and Jean would appreciate it. Maybe Gary has already done some research on this. Why don't you check with him, Cecily?"

Cecily nodded, and resolved to make work of this on Saturday, the only day when she would have time.

Finally Jason said, "As I suggested, let's discuss this topic next Sunday at our potluck."

*****

The following day was Wednesday, and Cecily phoned Gary to get an idea of what ministry he would like to follow on the mission field. A long silence greeted her question, and she began to think that he had found her intrusion into his affairs unwarranted, when he said, "Remember when we talked about doing something that has eternal value? Well, I am still trying to figure out what that could be, or how I could fit into such a mission program."

"Of course I remember. I think it's wonderful that you're trying to put God first in your life. I was asked to do some research on missionary agencies, especially on what they call "faith missions" to find out about their financial structures and how they function. Have you done any research yourself on the Internet?"

"Well, yes. I've looked up some agencies. Would you consider sharing your findings with me? I could use some help."

# Rejoicing in Hope

Cecily felt a warm glow in her heart.

"Yes, I'll be glad to do that. How about Saturday? I'll bring my laptop and we can work on it together."

Gary's voice sounded warmer. "Great. Where shall we work? Or would you rather work alone and then share your findings?"

Cecily knew she would much rather do the research with him than alone, but she only said, "We can do whatever you prefer. We can meet in Uncle Jason's office where we're not likely to be disturbed."

*****

On Sunday the three families met at the Nealey home, because they had a larger dining room and furniture to fill it. After they finished the meal, the children were put down to nap, and the adults settled down with their chosen beverages to discuss the financial practices of various "faith missions" and other Christian service organizations that worked overseas. While sharing their data, Gary quietly watched Cecily's usually serious face glow with animation. He had previously seen her as a dreamy, reflective girl, but now he was startled to notice that she had unusual beauty. A thought was born in his mind, but he quickly pushed it away. She was little more than a child and he was already approaching thirty. Switching his attention back to the topic at hand, he turned to Richard Kruyter.

"Does the translation organization to which you belong take engineers? What kind of ministry are they involved in?"

"As engineers they're support personnel and are involved in a construction type of ministry. They usually become involved in the local churches as well. However, they are encouraged to study some linguistics and anthropology before going to the field to help them in learning the language and culture of that field. Some of them

## Rejoicing in Hope

discover latent gifts in that area and turn to linguistic analysis and translation. We just had a pilot who switched to a language project and is very happy in it."

Gary's eyes brightened.

"You mean I could become a Bible translator, too?"

"You certainly could, if God leads you that way."

Gary let the thought take root in his mind, and he found the prospect inviting. *God, is this what you intend for me?*

Mike and Jean looked at each other, and some of their worries fell away. Listening to the Kruyters, they realized that some of their stereotypes of a "faith" missionary were simply wrong. Here were two people who were intellectually outstanding, spiritually inspiring, and personally attractive. The Ballards would be thankful to have their own intelligent son a part of such a group.

Mary and Jason looked on and smiled at each other. Jason remembered how strong Mary's ties were to the translation mission, and that she had been reluctant to sever those ties even for the love of her life.

*****

As June came to a close, the Kruyters began to pack for their return to Brazil. Gary had enrolled in the linguistics course in Dallas and would now work part time with his father's construction firm. He was very busy, and Cecily saw him only on Sundays at the potluck dinners. In church they were not even in the same Sunday school class: she was in the college-age class, and he was in the singles class. He was always courteous and friendly, but she saw no sign of any real interest in her, so she hid the ache in her heart.

After the Kruyters left, the Nealey house seemed empty. Mary had expected to relax from the stress the large household had imposed, but found that she was missing them

## Rejoicing in Hope

more than she had thought possible. She had more time to turn her attention to Cecily now, and began to wonder what burden her niece was carrying. Her expression was often sad rather than dreamy, but Mary did not like to invade her niece's privacy, so she simply prayed for her.

Meanwhile the Ballards became preoccupied with helping Carol plan her August wedding. She planned to marry in the final week of the month, and Cecily would have returned to Texarkana and college by that time. She would have liked to attend the wedding, but her ties with the couple were not so close that her absence would be noted. She and Paula were good friends, but she was barely acquainted with Carol.

# Rejoicing in Hope

# Rejoicing in Hope

## Chapter 7

The hot summer vacation in Dallas wore to a close and Cecily packed her cartons to return to Texarkana. This coming Sunday would be her last day in Cedar Hill. While she sorted her belongings she was wondering how she could encourage Gary. *Lord, you know how I feel about Gary. I don't think there's anything I can do for him, but please show him how much you love him.*

"Cecily!"

She heard her aunt's voice calling from the foot of the stairs.

"Yes, Aunt Mary?"

"Gary is here to see you, and asks if you can spare the time."

*If I can spare the time?* Cecily's heart pounded.

"I'll be right there."

She gave her reflection in the dresser mirror a quick glance, ran a brush through her hair, washed her hands, and prepared to descend the stairs.

Gary stood up from the couch and came to meet her.

"Mary said you were packing, and I don't want to hold you up, but I've seen so little of you lately that I thought I should come by to tell you how much I appreciate your encouragement."

Gary looked down into the large gray eyes that were glowing. He felt a lump in his throat. *Does she have any idea how beautiful she is?*

# Rejoicing in Hope

Cecily flushed. "I've wanted to tell you how much I admire you for putting God first in your life. Are you beginning to enjoy your studies?"

"Yes, I think I am. It kind of sneaked up on me. I'm starting to sense that this is what God means for my life. It's a privilege to be able to unlock the secrets of the gospel in a previously unwritten language!"

Cecily looked at him with something like envy. His face glowed and he looked like a man whose life had a purpose.

He went on, somewhat nervously, "Cecily, would you consider writing to me maybe once a month? We can communicate by e-mail, or by text messaging. I know you'll be busy in your senior year, but maybe we can encourage each other and keep in touch."

"I'd like that. Maybe you can help me find God's purpose for my life, too."

"It's a deal. I'd better go now." He turned and started for the door.

"Just a minute." Gary halted and looked back at her, waiting. She continued, "Are you planning to come to our potluck on Sunday?"

"I don't think I can." He was regretful. "I promised a friend I would have dinner with him on Sunday."

Cecily smiled. "I'm sorry, too," and put out her hand in farewell.

*****

Mary Nealey received a long letter from her friend Rachel Kruyter, who had returned to the adobe house in the reservation's access town.

"Cecily, I've got a letter from Rachel. Would you like to read it?"

# Rejoicing in Hope

"Does she write by 'snail-mail'? How long does it take for the letter to arrive here?"

"Yes, she writes by regular mail. Their electricity is very unpredictable, and she doesn't like to waste battery energy on personal letters unless there is urgency. The letters take about a week to ten days, sometimes longer."

Cecily held out her hand for the letter Mary was holding out to her. She slipped the letter out of its envelope, and read:

> Dear Mary and Jason,
>
> We arrived here safe and sound and were thankful to settle down again after all that traveling. Our *crente* (believer) friends kept watch over our house, and everything was in order. They even invited us to the first meal of rice and beans we've had in two months.
>
> I don't know whether you remember Belinda who taught me about Guará colors when we first arrived here; well, she was involved in a domestic incident in her village.
>
> Belinda is now in her late teens and has steadily refused to marry any of the young men who petitioned for her hand. Her uncle (her deceased father's brother) got worried that she was getting too old to marry (girls usually marry as soon as they enter puberty), so when a homely cross cousin (a marriageable relative) asked to marry her, her uncle was relieved, and consented.
>
> In such cases, my Guará friends tell me, the girl is informed, and is expected to concur. In this case, however, Belinda did *not*

# Rejoicing in Hope

concur, but her uncle told her it was final. She had to marry him.

When the young man presented himself at her uncle's home after dark, he was directed to Belinda's sapling-constructed bed. Belinda resolutely refused him, and then her uncle picked up a smoldering log from the fire and attacked her with it. She ran and he chased after her outdoors with the log that burst into flame.

The humiliated bridegroom told Belinda's uncle that the deal was off, and went back to his parent's hut.

Cecily could not help laughing, but sympathized with Belinda. *Imagine, being told you have to marry someone! Unless Uncle Jason or Daddy told me that I had to marry Gary. In that case I'd probably be glad to obey! What a world of difference between Belinda's would-be marriage and Carol Ballard's wedding!*

As Cecily loaded up her car for the return trip to Texarkana, she reflected that these weeks had been some of the happiest in her life, and now she could look forward to hearing from Gary. *I can hardly wait!*

*****

That evening Cecily observed that her father and brother were very happy to have her back. She had not expected the same reaction from her stepmother, who had never understood her. This was probably not altogether her fault, because Cecily had not been able to disguise her misgivings from the early days of their acquaintance. Cecily was old enough to remember her own mother's caresses, although she could not deny that her mother had been faithless as far as her husband was concerned. Still, Susan had little warmth

## Rejoicing in Hope

in her heart for her stepchildren. She had no children of her own, and whether that was by choice or by chance, Cecily never knew.

At suppertime the family drifted to the kitchen as was their custom and went to the well-stocked refrigerator and stove to choose from whatever food was there. Then they flocked to the den with their plates and ate while they watched television in silence. When they finished their plates they brought them to the kitchen and loaded them into the dishwasher. In Cecily's opinion, they "grazed" rather than "dined." Cecily remembered suppers at the Nealey home, where the family congregated at a large table and served themselves and others from bowls and platters before jointly bowing their heads in prayer to ask for a blessing on the food. After dessert they sat around to discuss whatever issue was on their hearts. When the Kruyters were there, the meals lasted an hour or longer, and were closed by reading Scripture and prayer. *When I have my own home, that's the way I want to live!*

After the news program was ended, Randy Sr. turned to his daughter.

"Let's turn off the TV and talk about what we've been doing all summer. We'll start with you, Susan," he said, turning to his wife.

"With me? I've been trying to keep this house neat and clean, shopping to keep us supplied with food, and kept myself busy with volunteer work all summer."

"What kind of volunteer work have you been doing, Susan?" Cecily tried to take a polite interest in her stepmother's activities.

"Twice a week I served at the shelter for homeless mothers and two days I helped serve dinner in the home for crippled veterans."

## Rejoicing in Hope

In spite of herself, Cecily was impressed. "That's great, Susan. That must make a big difference in those people's lives."

Susan sniffed. "I don't know about that. Most of them aren't very appreciative." Silence fell over the small group.

"And what have you been doing, Cecily?"

"I worked in Uncle Jason's office, keeping track of his appointments, keeping the books of income and expenditures, and helping Aunt Mary after work. She was super-busy with the missionary family who stayed with us the entire month of June. They had three young children."

"A missionary family?" Susan acted as though she had never heard of missionaries. "Where did they come from? What were they doing in Dallas?"

"They were friends of Aunt Mary's. She had been a partner of the wife in Brazil when they were both single. The Kruyters are translating the Bible for an Indian tribe out there. They were in Dallas to participate in a translation workshop."

"Why would they translate the Bible for Indians? The Bible is a very complicated book. There's no way a primitive tribe can understand it."

Cecily remembered with a shock that she had intended to ask that same question of her Aunt Mary, but somehow she had never gotten around to it. Her father interrupted:

"Before we get sidetracked, let's ask Randy Jr. what he did this summer. He's starting in college next week and then he'll move into the dorm."

Randy Jr. laughed. "I worked for a used car salesman. I washed and polished the cars that came in, and reported to the mechanic what I thought needed attention before we put it out for sale. The idea was to make it look as if the car was in good condition."

"Even if it wasn't really?" Cecily was skeptical.

"We sold them 'as is,' so the cars only had to look as if they were in good condition."

# Rejoicing in Hope

# Rejoicing in Hope

## Chapter 8

Cecily began her senior year in college. She received credit for the practical experience of the summer, working in her Uncle Jason's office. But as she enrolled in the courses she still needed to take in order to earn her degree, she began to struggle with the question of "how may I best serve the Lord?"

In her second week of the semester she received the long-awaited email message from Gary. She read and reread it so often that she virtually memorized it.

> Dear Cecily,
>
> I am sneaking some time away from my books to write you this note. Dallas doesn't seem the same since you went away. I miss you already and I hope you won't make me wait too long for an answer.
>
> I suppose you're expecting me to give you a report on Carol's wedding, but I'll only say that it was a big event. No doubt it cost Dad a pretty penny. Carol was very beautiful and very happy, so I guess that's what matters most. Paula met a friend of Jacob's (Carol's husband) at the rehearsal dinner, and they are now dating. I don't know much about him. I only know he is an accountant from Houston.
>
> Dad and Mom are becoming reconciled to the thought of my being a missionary. I think they were so deeply impressed with the

## Rejoicing in Hope

Kruyters that they no longer mind so much that I have chosen a ministry like theirs.

At the end of the year I am scheduled to take jungle survival training, and I'm looking forward to that. It will be a refreshing change from this solid dose of book and library studies. Every day I am more convinced that I made the right decision to become a Bible translator.

Don't wait too long before you answer.

Your friend,

Gary Ballard.

Cecily carefully folded up the note and slipped it into her pocket. Later that evening she returned to her room, turned on her computer, and sat down to answer his message.

Dear Gary,

It was great to receive your e-mail. I was promised that I will receive credit for my summer work, so that edges me closer to graduation.

I am wondering what I want to do after graduation, though. I'm keeping my options open. With a business major I can probably find work anywhere, including in mission administration.

You urged me not to wait too long to answer your message, but that means I will have a long wait—maybe as much as a month—before I can expect another message from you.

# Rejoicing in Hope

I have a Christian roommate this time, so that will be a nice change. She attends the same church I do. We also attend the same Intervarsity Christian Fellowship group. I think I will enjoy this year more than last.

Aunt Mary phones or emails me every week, and that's neat, too. I may go to Cedar Hill to spend Thanksgiving weekend with her. Do you have any plans for that weekend yet?

Randy Jr., my brother, is apparently enjoying his stay in the dorm. We communicate every week by email or text messaging. I am wondering how he will ever pass his subjects with all the "fun" he says he is having. I think the first year at college is the hardest, because most of us don't seem to know how to study when we finish high school.

No more news. I wait for your next message.

Cecily.

*****

Cecily was starting to feel guilty about the way she had neglected her grandmother. She had, of course, been away all during her summer vacation, and then came back just in time to take up her studies again. She determined to go home for a visit to see her grandmother. She sent an email to her father:

Dear Daddy,

I am thinking of coming home this weekend because I haven't visited Grandma since Easter weekend. I haven't heard how

## Rejoicing in Hope

she is doing, either, so I would like to come and see her. Will that be all right with Susan and you? Let me know ASAP.

Love,

Cecily.

She received a prompt affirmative answer and made her plans to visit her grandmother.

*****

She drove out to the Radcliffe Manor memory unit and found her grandmother sitting in a large room, surrounded by other elderly people, all of whom ignored everyone around them. Her grandmother looked at her briefly, almost with suspicion and uttered some garbled phrases, among which Cecily picked up the word "who." Assuming that she wanted to know who she was, Cecily said, "I'm your granddaughter, Cecily. I'm Randy's girl."

Mrs. Spears rambled on with more garbled words. Cecily noticed that her grandmother had lost a lot of weight and had aged a great deal since she had last seen her. She tried to converse with her, but noted with pain that her grandmother neither seemed to know her nor did she seem to understand anything Cecily said to her. When an aide came to wheel Mrs. Spears to a communal dining room, Cecily went along.

Three other patients were wheeled to the same small table. None of them seemed to connect with their colleagues around the table. They could have been on separate planets, for all the attention they paid to each other.

Mrs. Spears ignored the food on her plate. When Cecily spoke to her, she uttered her disconnected syllables. Cecily tried to feed her and slipped in a spoonful between her teeth

## Rejoicing in Hope

whenever she could. Often Mrs. Spears gritted her teeth and refused to admit the spoon.

After a few of Cecily's successful attempts at feeding her, Mrs. Spear reached into her mouth and pulled the food out with her fingers, and flung it away from her at random. Cecily decided to admit her defeat. She remembered reading that an Alzheimer's patient can often be reached by a childhood memory, so she began to hum a song that her grandmother had taught her when she was little:

> Lightly row, lightly row
> O'er the glassy waves we go;
> Smoothly glide, smoothly glide,
> O'er the silent tide.
> Let the winds and waters be
> Mingled with our melody;
> Sing and float, sing and float,
> In our little boat.

Cecily was startled at the silence that suddenly fell on the dining room. Then she heard several people begin to sing the song. She sang along with them, and noticed that her grandmother joined them.

When they finished she hugged her grandmother, and felt her grandmother return her embrace. She looked into her bleary eyes, and saw that the old song had made contact with her. Tears came in Cecily's eyes, and she silently thanked God.

When she arrived at her father's home she joined him in the den. He looked up from his newspaper and said, "Have you seen your grandma? How was she?"

"When was the last time you visited her, Dad?"

"A month ago," he admitted. "How is she?"

## Rejoicing in Hope

"She changed so much since I last saw her, Daddy. She couldn't even speak a logical sentence, and she didn't seem to know me at all. At meal time she didn't feed herself. I tried to feed her, but she didn't let much into her mouth."

Randy Senior nodded. "She has deteriorated a lot. I don't know if there's anything sadder than dementia."

*****

Cecily returned to her college dorm after that disappointing visit with her grandmother. She threw herself into her studies and began praying very seriously about what she should do after college. She also hoped against hope that Gary would send her an email before the month was up. She was not interested in dating anyone on campus, but one young man who was active in the Intervarsity Christian Fellowship had been quite persistent in asking her out. Because she was lonely, she relented. She accompanied Robert to several social outings.

Coming home from one of the outings promoted by the Fellowship she found an email from Gary. She printed it out and sat down to enjoy it at her leisure.

Dear Cecily,

I received your last message, which was very brief. It's hard to imagine what you are thinking and dreaming of when you write such terse messages.

I am doing well and this past week the director of the Brazil Branch of the Bible Translators Mission was in town, and asked to talk to any of the students who might be interested in language work in that huge country. Remembering Richard's and Rachel's reports of their work, I decided to sign up for an interview.

# Rejoicing in Hope

Well, I got in to see him and was very favorably impressed with him. He told me about some of the Indian tribes that live in a refuge designated for them in the Xingú River region. Foreign missionaries are denied access to them, because the country's social scientists are trying to prevent culture change being imposed on them from the outside.

Well, it's not hard to keep missionaries out, because they tend to be law-abiding people, but keeping the Indians in, so that they have no contact with the missionaries is not so easy. So the current missionary strategy is to establish themselves in access towns where the Indians visit. Several of the translation teams have settled in different access towns to welcome the Indian visitors, learn their languages, and witness to them of God's love for them. It's the kind of ministry that is not publicized, but surely needs our prayers. I feel strongly drawn to do this kind of work.

Before we know it Thanksgiving will be here. I hope you're planning to visit your Aunt Mary over that weekend. Would you like me to drive up there and pick you up at your college? Just tell me when and where. I'll be there.

Gary

# Rejoicing in Hope

# Rejoicing in Hope

## Chapter 9

In November Cecily received a call from her father. He told her that her grandmother was failing rapidly, and that he had put her in hospice care because the doctor thought she had less than six months to live. Randy Sr. thought that she was unlikely to live that long, so he urged his daughter to find time to visit her grandmother before Thanksgiving, if possible. He said he had issued the same call to Randy Jr. Cecily promised to drive out to see her that very weekend, if possible.

After she hung up, her thoughts were troubled. Was her grandmother a Christian? She never attended church. She had taken her grandchildren to church once at their request, but other than that one time, she knew of no other. She did not pray, as far as Cecily knew. Would she be going into eternity without Christ? She shared her burden with her roommate and other friends of the Intervarsity Christian Fellowship. They promised to pray with urgency.

She drove home that weekend and went directly to her father's office. He welcomed her and showed his relief at her prompt response.

"Daddy, can you tell me something about Grandma? Did she ever attend church? Was she religious when she was young? What was your father like?"

Her father urged her to sit down, and pulled up a chair beside her.

"When your grandma was young, just about everybody went to church. She was no exception. She took us to Sunday school every Sunday. But everything changed when my father (your grandpa) abandoned the family and took off with a pretty young girl. He left my mother with a pile of

## Rejoicing in Hope

debts and three children to support. She turned to the church for help, and the minister suggested to her that she was probably to blame, that Dad would not have run off with another woman if she had satisfied his needs. She was so hurt that she turned her back on the church."

"Oh Daddy, how awful! Poor Grandma!"

Randy Sr. nodded.

"Have you asked a chaplain to visit her, to help her in this final phase of her life?"

Her father shook his head. "You know that she seems completely out of contact, so I couldn't ask anyone to do that."

"Do you have one of Grandma's old hymnbooks stored away somewhere, Daddy?"

Randy Sr. showed his surprise. "I stored some of her things away at home when I moved her into Radcliffe Manor. Why don't you ask Susan to show you where Grandma's books are stored?"

Cecily thanked her father and parted from him with a hug. She went home, but not finding Susan there, she went up into the attic and found some dusty boxes that she recognized as containing some of her grandmother's belongings. She picked out a hymnbook from of one of the boxes, dusted it off, and headed toward the Radcliffe Manor's Hospice section. She had an idea, based on her experience with the children's song she had sung the last time she was there.

She found her grandmother in a pleasantly furnished room she shared with another woman. The room was well lighted and airy. She pulled up a chair to her grandmother's bed and began to talk to her. She talked about events in her own childhood after she and her brother had been moved

## Rejoicing in Hope

into her grandmother's house. At first her grandmother's eyes remained unfocussed, but gradually Cecily thought she could notice a change in awareness. Then she began to sing a children's hymn from the old hymnbook, one that old Mrs. Spears probably sang as a child:

> Jesus loves me, this I know
> For the Bible tells me so.
> Little ones to him belong,
> They are weak, but he is strong.
> Yes, Jesus loves me,
> Yes, Jesus loves me,
> Yes, Jesus loves me:
> The Bible tells me so.

She thought that Mrs. Spears was looking more alert, so she sang two more stanzas of the same hymn:

> Jesus loves me, he who died
> Heaven's gate to open wide;
> He will wash away my sin
> Let his little child come in.

> Jesus loves me, he will stay
> Close beside me all the way;
> He prepared a home for me
> And someday his face I'll see.

> Yes, Jesus loves me,
> Yes, Jesus loves me.
> Yes, Jesus loves me,
> The Bible tells me so.[1]

On the final stanza and chorus Cecily saw Mrs. Spears' lips moving as she accompanied the song. Cecily searched in the old book for another hymn, of which she knew very few. The Intervarsity group sang mostly choruses, and Cecily

---

[1] Anna B. Warner

## Rejoicing in Hope

knew that her grandmother would not know any of them. She began to sing softly:

> What a Friend we have in Jesus,
> All our sins and griefs to bear!
> What a privilege to carry
> Everything to God in prayer!
> O what peace we often forfeit,
> O what needless pain we bear,
> All because we do not carry
> Everything to God in prayer!
>
> Have we trials and temptations?
> Is there trouble anywhere?
> We should never be discouraged—
> Take it to the Lord in prayer.
> Can we find a friend so faithful
> Who will all our sorrows share?
> Jesus knows our every weakness—
> Take it to the Lord in prayer.
>
> Are we weak and heavy laden,
> Cumbered with a load of care?
> Precious Savior, still our refuge—
> Take it to the Lord in prayer.
> Do thy friends despise, forsake thee?
> Take it to the Lord in prayer;
> In his arms he'll take and shield thee—
> Thou wilt find a solace there.[1]

Cecily saw tears sparkling in her grandmother's eyes and the tears rose in her own eyes. She stood up and bent over her grandmother's bed, throwing her arms around her, praying audibly:

"Lord, please take my grandmother in your arms and show her that you love her and forgive her for all the years

---
[1] Joseph Scriven

## Rejoicing in Hope

she turned her back on you. Show her that she has never had a better Friend than you have been to her, her whole life long."

She heard her grandmother breathe, "Cecily!" and answered, "Yes, Grandma, it's me."

# Rejoicing in Hope

# Rejoicing in Hope

## Chapter 10

Two days before Thanksgiving she received a call from Gary on her cell phone.

"Your Aunt Mary is expecting you for Thanksgiving. Will you be able to make it?"

"I'm not sure." Cecily was divided between her joy at receiving a call from Gary, and her disappointment that she would not be able to see him. "My Grandma is failing fast, and I don't want her to die alone. I had planned to drive down to Cedar Hill, and I want to very much, but I think I should be with Grandma when her time comes."

There was a long silence on the telephone.

"How about it if I drive up there instead to spend Thanksgiving with you? Would that be possible?"

"I guess so." Cecily wondered what her parents would say about having a guest on such short notice. "I think I should ask my folks about that first."

There was another long silence. She could almost hear Gary's doubts during this pause. "Why don't you do that? Unless you have other plans."

"No, as I told you, I had planned to spend Thanksgiving weekend in Cedar Hill, but now I think I would always be sorry if I couldn't be with Grandma when she goes. She has always been there for me, as long as she was able. You see, I don't know if she is a Christian or not, and I wouldn't want her to die without someone to point her to Christ."

"Of course. Why don't you talk to your parents and let me know what they decide. It they decide no, I'll come up with an alternative."

# Rejoicing in Hope

After Cecily hung up, she wondered whether Gary thought that she was trying to get out of it. She was almost certain that Susan would dislike having a stranger in the house, and she wasn't sure what her father would think. *After all, I'm not even dating Gary. Won't Daddy think it strange to have Gary come to visit us over a family holiday?*

*****

That evening she phoned her father. She asked him how her grandmother was, and he replied that he had visited her that very day and she was definitely failing. She was calmer than previously, and she had responded briefly to his hugs and greetings. When he told her that Cecily would be coming that weekend, she actually had almost smiled.

"I think it means a lot to her when you visit. The nurse said she seems more relaxed, but she's no longer eating so it won't be long any more."

"Daddy, a friend of mine from Cedar Hill would like to come here to pass Thanksgiving with us, since I won't be going there. Would that be all right?"

"Of course. We'll be happy to have her come."

Cecily felt herself flushing.

"It's a 'he,' Daddy, and not a 'she.' Is that a problem?"

Randy Sr. quickly corrected himself.

"Of course not. He can share Randy Jr.'s room. I'll warn Randy."

Cecily thanked him and hung up the phone.

*****

When Cecily arrived home the day before Thanksgiving, and turned into her father's driveway, she saw another car

# Rejoicing in Hope

parked on the approach to the garage. *Can this be Gary's car?*

She was still hurting from her last encounter with Robert. He had asked if he might visit her at home, and she had said no. She told him she was staying with her father so that she could be with her grandmother, who was dying. He had looked puzzled.

"But you won't be with her all day, will you?"

"No, I suppose not." Cecily wondered how she could let him understand that a visit from him would be inconvenient at this time. "A friend is coming from Cedar Hill to spend the weekend with us, and this is not a good time for more guests."

"What if I come on Saturday afternoon? I would like to meet your family."

"I don't think so. I want to spend time with my grandmother. She brought me up and I owe her that attention."

Robert looked disappointed and unconvinced, but said no more.

*That looks like Gary's car. I feel awkward about fending off Robert's attentions. I am more interested in Gary than anyone else, but we're not going steady, not even dating, or anything. I just think he is the most wonderful man I know, but he has given me no real reason to think he is thinking of me in that way. How can I explain this to Robert? I can't.* She shrugged her shoulders.

She parked her car behind Gary's and slowly got out. As she neared the front door, it opened, and Gary came out to greet her. He held out both hands, and she placed hers in his. She avoided meeting his eyes and struggled to swallow the lump in her throat.

# Rejoicing in Hope

"Cecily! You look wonderful! It's great to see you. Thanks for letting me come to see you."

"It's great to see you, too. You know that I want to be with my grandmother, don't you?"

Gary's voice took on a tender note. "Yes, I know. I thought maybe I could sit with you while you watch at your grandma's bed. We can join in praying for her."

They turned and Gary helped her to remove the baggage from her trunk and carry it into the house.

*****

True to his offer, Gary accompanied Cecily to the hospice where her grandmother lay hovering between unconsciousness and awareness. Cecily greeted her grandmother and talked to her about the weather and Randy's exploits in college. Gradually her grandmother began to respond by following Cecily with her eyes. Then Cecily introduced Gary to her as "a friend from Cedar Hill." Gary came up to the bed, took Mrs. Spears' hand in his, and told her he was happy to meet her, because she was so important to Cecily. Mrs. Spears focused her eyes on him while he talked to her.

Gary quoted some familiar Bible passages to her. He began with the twenty-third Psalm:

> The Lord is my shepherd, I shall not want.
> He maketh me to lie down in green pastures:
> he leadeth me beside the still waters.
> He restoreth my soul: he leadeth me in paths
> of righteousness for his name's sake.
> Yea, though I walk through the valley of the
> shadow of death, I will fear no evil: for thou
> art with me; thy rod and thy staff they comfort
> me.

# Rejoicing in Hope

> Thou preparest a table before me in the presence of mine enemies: Thou anointest my head with oil, my cup runneth over.
> Surely goodness and love shall follow me all the days of my life: and I will dwell in the house of the Lord forever.[1]

Cecily watched with wonder as her grandmother's lips moved along with Gary's narration of the old familiar psalm. Then Gary pulled a small leather book out of his pocket, and read the thirty-second Psalm to her:

> Blessed is he whose transgressions are forgiven, whose sins are covered.
> Blessed is the man whose sin the Lord does not count against him and in whose spirit is no deceit.
> When I kept silent, my bones wasted away through my groaning all day long.
> For day and night your hand was heavy upon me; my strength was sapped as in the heat of summer.
> Then I acknowledged my sin to you and did not cover up my iniquity.
> I said, "I will confess my transgression to the Lord"—and you forgave the guilt of my sin.
> Therefore let everyone who is godly pray to you while you may be found; surely when the mighty waters rise, they will not reach him.
> You are my hiding place; you will protect me from trouble and surround me with songs of deliverance.[2]

Cecily saw tears roll down her grandmother's cheeks. She knelt beside the bed and took her grandmother's hand in

---

[1] Psalm 23:1-6, KJV
[2] Psalm 32:1-7

## Rejoicing in Hope

her own. She read one of her favorite psalms from the Bible she held in her hands:

> Praise the Lord O my soul; all my inmost being, praise his holy name.
>
> Praise the Lord, O my soul, and forget not all his benefits—who forgives all your sins and heals all your diseases, who redeems your life from the pit and crowns you with love and compassion, who satisfies your desires with good things so that your youth is renewed like the eagle's.
>
> The Lord works righteousness and justice for all the oppressed.
>
> He made known his ways to Moses, his deeds to the people of Israel: The Lord is compassionate and gracious, slow to anger, abounding in love.
>
> He will not always accuse, nor will he harbor his anger forever; he does not treat us as our sins deserve or repay us according to our iniquities.
>
> For as high as the heavens are above the earth, so great is his love for those who fear him; as far as the east is from the west, so far has he removed our transgressions from us.
>
> As a father has compassion on his children, so the Lord has compassion on those who fear him; for he knows how we are formed, he remembers that we are dust.[1]

Mrs. Spears sighed and closed her eyes. Cecily bowed her head and prayed: "Lord, you know what's going on in Grandma's heart. Thank you for your mercy that reaches out

---

[1] Psalm 103:1-14

## Rejoicing in Hope

to us our whole lives long. Please forgive her and bring peace to her heart."

# Rejoicing in Hope

# Rejoicing in Hope

## Chapter 11

Early on Thanksgiving morning Cecily entered the dining room to find her father speaking on the phone. Judging by the seriousness of his aspect, she guessed that it was not a social call. As he carefully put the receiver back in place, he turned to her.

"That was the Hospice. Your grandma passed away early this morning."

Cecily's face mirrored the shock she felt.

"She died?"

"Yes, just about 45 minutes ago. The nurse found her when she made her rounds this morning. She had just passed away, because her body was still warm."

Cecily groped for a chair and sat down.

"I never thought…." She looked at her father. "Does that mean that she was alone when she died?"

Randy Sr. put an arm around her shoulders. "It looks like it. I stopped by last night before midnight and she was not responding at all. I think she must have slipped into unconsciousness shortly after you left last night."

At that moment Gary came into the room, and looking from one face to the other, he asked, "Bad news?"

Cecily turned around and headed for the stairs. Gary tried to stop her to ask what was wrong, but her father gestured for him to leave her go. Gary hesitated, and dropped his hand. Cecily touched his arm as if to apologize, and turned toward the stairs. She could hear her father explain

# Rejoicing in Hope

about her grandmother's death as she climbed toward her room.

\*\*\*\*\*

Cecily emerged from her room an hour later. She found Gary sitting in the living room, reading the morning paper. He folded it up when he noticed that she had come in and stood up to greet her.

"How is everything?" The words were casual, but the look in his eyes was not.

She smiled wanly. "It's just that I didn't expect her to go so soon. I thought she was responding to the verses we read to her, and now she is gone already." She gestured vaguely with her hand. "I can't help wondering how much she understood of what we tried to tell her."

"Remember that it wasn't the first time she heard the gospel. From what your dad tells me, she was raised in a Bible-believing home, so she probably understood the implications of the verses we read to her. For the rest, we can only leave her in God's hands."

Cecily nodded. She knew he was right. Only she wished so much that she could be sure that her grandmother was safe with the Lord. She reached out and accepted the hand he held out to her.

\*\*\*\*\*

On Thanksgiving Day the Spears family ate at one of the few restaurants in Texarkana that was open on that holiday. Randy Junior had invited an out-of-state student from his dorm to the meal, and Gary joined the family as Cecily's guest.

Cecily had expected the meal to be a solemn affair, with her grandmother's death on everyone's mind, but Randy

## Rejoicing in Hope

Junior reminded her of the realities of their grandmother's death.

"It isn't as if we'll be missing her, because she he hasn't been with us for a long time now. She's been gone for over six months. It's that long since she knew any of us."

Cecily admitted the logic. It wasn't that she missed her grandmother, but she felt the pain of her passing. *If only I knew whether she has gone to be with the Lord! There is nothing I can do about it now, but I wish I had spent more time visiting her, reminding her of the Lord and his love.*

*****

The funeral was held the day after Thanksgiving. Her father wanted the pastor of a large wealthy church to perform the memorial service, but Cecily protested. She wanted a message that would eulogize the Lord for what he had done, rather than her grandmother, although she knew she would always be grateful for what her grandmother had done for her brother and herself. They compromised by inviting both this pastor and the elderly pastor from a small church who was well-known in the community for his prison ministry. Gary planned to leave immediately after the funeral, because his classes began on Monday.

The funeral home filled up with many elderly people who had known old Mrs. Spears for years. Gary Ballard stood with Cecily, and was introduced as a friend she had met in Dallas that summer. Susan Spears received the guests with her husband, and Randy Junior alternately stood with his parents and with Cecily.

At the close of the formalities, Gary pressed her arm and reminded her that he had to leave. She urged him to partake of the lunch first, which he agreed to do. They had little opportunity to speak privately, but as they sat at a small table

## Rejoicing in Hope

together, she tried to thank him for coming, and apologized for spending so little time with him.

Gary smiled. "We didn't have much time to talk, but I'm glad I had this opportunity to be with you and share the last moments you had with your grandmother. Don't forget to write, and don't wait too long before you do."

Cecily shyly smiled her thanks. "I will. You helped me a lot through these days. I can't thank you enough."

Gary's look was sober. "I'm making plans to go to Mexico for jungle survival training, probably in February. Meanwhile, I need to establish some kind of support base before I go."

Cecily wondered what a "support base" was, and how he would "establish" it. They were interrupted by the people who were preparing to leave and wanted to say goodbye to the members of the Spears family, and so Cecily merely had time to hug Gary and respond to his gentle kiss with a shy one.

Gary was gone before she was fully aware of it.

*****

Cecily returned to her college dormitory the following day. In the days that followed she gradually became aware of the grief she felt at her grandmother's passing. She realized that her brother Randy Junior was right: to some extent she had already lost her grandmother when the latter developed the dementia symptoms, but her death made the loss irrevocable. With the passing of her grandmother there was less to tie her to Texarkana, although her relationship with her father had always been excellent. Somehow she felt like an intruder in her stepmother's home. She did not want to offend her father by letting him know how estranged she felt in his home, but it was no longer hers.

# Rejoicing in Hope

Four days after she returned to college she received a message from Gary:

Dear Cecily,

Somehow heaven seems so much closer now that we were able to walk with your grandmother a little way on her path. I don't know whether she turned to the Lord in her final hours or not, but I do know that God sent us there to give her the final message of grace. That was a great privilege.

This experience has made me more aware than ever of the many millions of people who are still waiting for the gospel, facing death and eternity without the Lord. How I pray that God will allow me to bring his Word to some people group that has never heard the gospel before! What a wonderful message of grace and forgiveness we have! We need to bring it to those who have yet to hear.

Have you ever considered becoming a missionary, Cecily? Have you ever sensed that the Lord is calling you to bring his Word to those who have never heard? Isaiah wrote:

"How beautiful on the mountains are the feet of those who bring good news, who proclaim peace, who bring good tidings, who proclaim salvation, who say to Zion, 'Your God reigns!'"[1]

I have joined the jail evangelism team at church, and am excited about the opportunity to share the good news with the prisoners.

---

[1] Isaiah 52:7

## Rejoicing in Hope

I told your Aunt Mary about your grandmother, and she was sorry she didn't know about her death. She would have liked to attend the funeral. I felt ashamed that I never thought about telling her.

Here at home all seems to be peaceful. All, that is, except for a spat between Carol and her new husband. But I guess that happens in the best of families.

Paula and her accountant are still dating, although they only see each other a couple times a month.

I am enclosing a copy of a letter from Rachel Kruyter. Her letters are always interesting.

Write me soon and tell me what is going on with you.

Gary.

Cecily read the message with mixed feelings. She felt something like dismay as she realized that Gary was far ahead of her spiritually, and she had to admit she thought of missionary work reluctantly, and had tried to dismiss it from her mind. *I could never do that kind of work. You have to be brave and outgoing; you have to be really spiritual to be a missionary. I'm too shy and timid. I'd be willing to do it with Gary, but not alone; not as a single woman.* At the same time she felt something like pride in Gary, for his lofty aspirations.

Cecily downloaded the attachment which contained Rachel's letter to her Aunt Mary, and read:

I just received the following message from Rachel:

# Rejoicing in Hope

I don't know if I told you that I decided to raise chickens so that we can have our own supply of eggs and meat. It seemed like a good idea and should have been very simple to do. All they need is a place off the ground to roost at night, and some corn to supplement the bugs and seeds they eat on their own. We bought ten chickens from an *ãyuhuk* (non-Indian) rancher and figured that would do for us. Richard put up a little shelter where the hens can roost at night, and we were in business.

Alas, somehow we failed to take the entrepreneurship of the Guará boys into account. After a few days I counted the hens, and we only had seven left. What happened to the hens?

The usual procedure is that the Indians come to the front door of our house to ask for medicines, which I keep in our *sala*. I count out the pills carefully for them in the *sala*, and then go to the front room where the Indian mothers are waiting for me, to give instructions on how they should use the medication. I began to notice that the boys who accompanied the women wore sly expressions of enjoyment while the women waited to receive the doled-out medicines. At sundown that day only five hens came home to roost.

As I confided my suspicions to Richard, he thought I was unduly distrustful.

# Rejoicing in Hope

"Probably the Indian dogs have killed a few, or maybe they just strayed away," he suggested.

I was not convinced. When the next group of Indians came to ask for medicines, I pretended to fill the tiny envelopes, but peered out of the corner of a kitchen window, and, sure enough—there were two boys creeping in the tall grass, looking for the hens that were feeding there. I saw one boy seize a hen and run away with it.

What could we do? We could refuse to treat the Indians, but that would probably make the innocent suffer more than the guilty. I was furious, but decided that raising chickens is out, at least for the time being.

Love,

Rachel

# Rejoicing in Hope

## Chapter 12

The year-end holidays were approaching and Cecily accepted her aunt's invitation to spend the holidays in Cedar Hill. Randy Junior was spending Christmas with his college roommate, and this meant that her father and stepmother would be alone during most of the vacation. When Cecily expressed her regret to her father, he smiled.

"You mean you would prefer to spend Christmas with me rather than with Gary?"

Cecily blushed. "Not exactly, but I don't like to think of you spending Christmas alone here."

Her father teased, "Not quite alone, after all, your stepmother will be here with me." He noticed the expression on her face, which she hastened to control and she managed to smile at her father.

"You know what I mean, Daddy. I mean alone without either of your kids."

Randy's face became sober. "I'll miss you both very much. It won't seem like Christmas without any kids."

"Would you like me to stay, Daddy?" She didn't know whether her father was serious or not. Did he wish her to stay?

"I think you should stay with me on Christmas holidays until you're an old lady." Then he laughed. "It's normal for kids to grow up and form their own families. That's the way it goes. Go to your aunt Mary's and have a wonderful time."

*****

# Rejoicing in Hope

December 20 found Cecily driving down Interstate 30, headed for Cedar Hill. She sang along with her CD player, her heart light as a feather. She was filled with anticipation at the prospect of spending two weeks with her aunt and uncle, and most of that time, with Gary.

Only last week Gary had e-mailed her, and had repeated his question from an earlier message: had Cecily ever considered becoming a missionary? She had avoided answering that part of his earlier message, and put the question about a career on the mission field aside. She found the issue too intimidating, too frightening.

She was a city girl and could not imagine herself living in primitive situations with preliterate people. Gary was enthused about the prospect, but Cecily could not imagine it for herself. *Yet if it's so important to Gary, should I consider it?*

Today, however, Cecily could only think about seeing Gary in a few hours. As she neared the Dallas-Fort Worth area, she remembered the happy hours she had spent there during the summer.

As she entered the driveway of the Nealey home, her Aunt Mary came out of the house to greet her. She had wrapped a jacket around her shoulders to protect herself from the gusty Texas wind. Now she hugged Cecily and told her how happy she was to see her. She helped her niece carry her baggage into the house and invited her to join her in the kitchen for a cup of coffee.

As they seated themselves cozily at the kitchen table, Mary told her niece some of the family news.

"Carol is expecting, and the Ballards are delighted at the prospect of a grandchild. You can imagine! Paula just became engaged to her CPA, but they probably won't marry until Paula graduates."

# Rejoicing in Hope

"What about Gary? Is he still studying?"

"No, Gary is traveling on deputation or what they now call 'partnership development.' He received several invitations from Michigan and Iowa churches to speak. I'm sure that it must be the Kruyters who have recommended him. Anyway, he's in Grand Rapids this week, and won't be back until the twenty-fourth, Christmas Eve."

Cecily's heart sank. He had said nothing about this in his latest email. *Was this what he meant when he spoke about "raising his support base"? Is he traveling and speaking to raise money for his jungle survival course?* Cecily swallowed the lump in her throat and wildly searched for something to say to cover up her disappointment.

"Have the Ballards accepted the idea of Gary going to the mission field?"

"Partly. They're proud of him, of course, but they won't be happy to see him go. They had high career hopes for him, you know."

Cecily nodded. They sat in silence for several minutes, and then Cecily said, "If you have nothing planned for me, Aunt Mary, I think I would like to take a little nap. I just turned in my last term papers this morning."

"Of course. Let me help you carry your cases upstairs and then you can settle down for a nap. The house will be quiet, because Jason took Jay shopping this afternoon, to buy something for Mommy."

Cecily stood up and picked up two cases. She was relieved that she could have the privacy she needed to struggle with her disappointment.

*****

Cecily's emotions were divided between bitter disappointment and anger. *How can Gary decide to become*

# Rejoicing in Hope

*a missionary without even asking how I feel about it? Does that mean that I'm not important to him after all?* She paced in the room, trying to conquer her feelings. Then she remembered that he *had* been asking her how she felt about becoming a missionary, but she had chosen to ignore his question.

*Am I getting in the way of what God is doing in Gary's life? Isn't he supposed to consider God's will more important than mine?*

Cecily stopped pacing, and threw herself on the bed. "Oh God, what can I do? I love Gary, but I don't think I could face being a missionary and living like the Kruyters do. I don't know what to do."

*****

Cecily woke up to find the room dark, and the short winter day was coming to an end. She got up, washed her face and brushed her hair, and decided to talk to her Aunt Mary.

As she descended the stairs she could smell the aroma of beef brisket and she heard the excited voice of her little cousin Jay, who had come home from his Christmas shopping trip. He was trying to tell his mother what he had bought for her, while his father tried to persuade him to keep it a secret until Christmas Day. Cecily could not help smiling.

Mary greeted her niece and asked if she was hungry. Cecily admitted that she was ravenous. Bread was cooling on the counter, fresh and fragrant from the bread maker. She greeted her Uncle Jason and little Jay, and followed Mary into the kitchen to help her by setting the table in the dining room. She brought the meat platter to the table, along with the salad and bean casserole, while Mary finished making the gravy.

## Rejoicing in Hope

"Paula will be here shortly. Her fiancé Kevin will be coming Christmas Eve to visit the Ballards. Paula spent Thanksgiving with Kevin's family."

Mary scrutinized Cecily's face, and tried to decide whether she had any business talking to Cecily about Gary's plans. After hesitating, she asked, "Are you happy that Gary plans to go to the mission field?"

Cecily felt the tears burn in her eyes.

"No, I can't feel happy about that."

Mary stirred the brown gravy that was bubbling on the stove, and turned to face her niece.

"You know that he loves you, don't you?"

"I hoped he did, but it looks as though he's not planning on any life with me."

"Do you want him to ignore God's call on his life so that he can marry you?"

Cecily was shocked. "Of course not. It's only that he hasn't consulted me about it. It's just as if what I want doesn't matter at all."

Mary's face became serious. "Are you sure of that? Hasn't he said anything to you about his plans to become a missionary? Hasn't he asked whether you're willing to serve the Lord overseas? He needs to know."

"But I'm not really willing, because I'm not brave enough nor outgoing enough to face a life among savage people. I just can't imagine living like that!"

"Let me turn off the stove, and then let's pray right here that the Lord will make you willing to be willing to serve him wherever he leads."

## Rejoicing in Hope

They both knelt on the kitchen floor, and Mary led in prayer for Cecily to yield to God's will for her life. Cecily struggled against the urge to burst into tears.

# Rejoicing in Hope

## Chapter 13

After supper Paula and Cecily did the dishes, while Mary put little Jay to bed. Paula was eager to talk about Kevin and their plans for a future together. Cecily was envious. How wonderful it would be if she and Gary could plan for an ordinary future together. But she shared Paula's excitement as sincerely as she could.

When they finished in the kitchen, Paula announced that she had to go home, but invited Cecily to have supper with the Ballard family the following evening. Cecily hesitated, unsure whether she would be imposing on the family under false pretenses.

"I don't know whether I should," she began, but Paula interrupted by speaking to Mary, who had just entered the living room.

"Do encourage Cecily to visit us," Paula begged. "We seldom get to see her."

Mary agreed. "Why don't you go, Cecily? You'll enjoy getting better acquainted with the family."

Cecily reluctantly consented.

*****

When Cecily retired to her room that evening, she was assaulted by doubts. She remembered her Aunt Mary's exhortation: "...let's pray that the Lord will make you willing to be willing to serve him wherever he leads." Cecily knelt beside her bed and confessed, "God, I know I asked you to make my life worthwhile, but I didn't mean that I would be willing to go to the mission field. Can't I do something worthwhile and stay in Texas?"

# Rejoicing in Hope

From somewhere in her memory the words of an early prayer echoed in her heart: "Lord, I want you to take over my life and make something worthwhile out of it."

Cecily sobbed.

"I don't really want to be a missionary, God. I know I ought to want to, but I don't. I know I don't deserve anyone as good as Gary, yet I wouldn't love him so much if he didn't love you so much. Change me, Lord, and make me into the kind of person you want me to be."

A peace settled in her heart, and she got ready for bed.

*****

The following day Mary took both Paula and Cecily Christmas shopping. The mall presented a festive aspect with its decorations and piped-in Christmas carols.

After a satisfying day of browsing in some of their favorite stores, Mary dropped the two young women off at the Ballard home. With some trepidation Cecily followed Paula into the house.

Paula's mother was busy in the kitchen, but paused to greet Cecily warmly. Cecily offered to help her with something in the kitchen, but Jean assured her that she had everything organized. "Why don't you just sit down in that chair and talk to me?"

Cecily obediently took off her jacket and hung it over the back of the kitchen chair. She sat down and admired Jean's decorative arrangement of the kitchen while Paula competently set the table. The walls were taupe, with a bright floral trim along the top of the wall.

"When do you need to be back in the dorm, Cecily?" Jean's question took her guest by surprise.

# Rejoicing in Hope

"The first Tuesday after New Year's Day. Classes begin on Wednesday."

"Will you be going home before heading out to the college? I'm asking because I'm hoping you can stay until after New Year's Day," Jean explained.

"I wasn't planning to do more than pick up my things that I left at home. My father doesn't expect me to stay there, and my stepmother has her hands full with all the volunteer work she does in the community."

Jean paused to lift the sweet potatoes out of the pan and into a bowl.

"We're expecting Gary by Christmas Eve. We're hoping he'll phone us tonight to tell us more exactly when he can be here. We realize that this may be the last Christmas he'll spend with us for several years."

Cecily was surprised. "How long will his survival training take? I thought it was only three months."

"True. But after that training period he'll be traveling around to raise his support, and then he hopes to go to Brazil as soon as he has raised his support quota. He probably won't be with us next Christmas, if all goes as he plans."

Cecily felt an ache in her heart. She watched Jean lift the ham out of the roasting pan, and stir the gravy from the drippings.

"Did you say he'll phone tonight?" Cecily wanted a chance to tell him that she had turned her life over to the Lord, to go wherever he wanted her to go. *Like Gary, I want my life to have eternal meaning.*

The back door opened and Mike entered. He greeted his wife with a kiss, and shook hands with Cecily. He patted Paula's back while she filled the glasses with ice water.

# Rejoicing in Hope

The phone rang, and Paula rushed to answer it. It was Kevin, so she laid the receiver down to take up the extension in the living room.

Jean smiled as she hung up the kitchen phone. "We'll just go ahead and start supper, because Paula will probably be on the phone for a while."

*****

After supper Paula and Cecily cleared away the dishes and stacked them in the dishwasher. While they were doing this the telephone rang, and the third ring was cut short, meaning that someone had answered the phone from an extension. Cecily tensed, wondering if that could be Gary calling. She was waiting to be summoned, but no one called her. She continued with the work of tidying up the kitchen.

After five minutes, Cecily heard Jean call her name. She rushed to the living room, to find Jean holding out the telephone receiver to her. "It's Gary, Cecily."

"Hello. This is Cecily speaking." She heard Gary chuckle.

"It's just me, Cecily. I was planning to phone you at Mary's house, but Mom says you had supper with the family tonight, so I get to talk to you now. How are you enjoying your Christmas vacation?"

"I just arrived yesterday, and have been having a wonderful time. How about you?"

"I've been very busy. I spoke at a men's Bible study, at a Ladies' Aid meeting, and at a youth retreat last week. This week I spoke to a Sunday school class, and to a young people's meeting. I had a wonderful time, but will be glad to find myself home again. How long are you planning to stay in Cedar Hill?"

"I was planning to stay until after New Year's."

# Rejoicing in Hope

"Great! I should be home tomorrow. I'm traveling on standby, so I can't say exactly when I'll arrive. Anyway, I hope to see you then. How have things been going for you?"

Cecily groped for the words to tell him of her changed attitude toward mission work. "I've been considering what I should do after college, and I came to the decision that I want my life to count for something."

There was silence on Gary's end, and then he asked, "What does that mean? Does that mean you're willing to go into missionary work, or that you're not willing?"

"It means that I want to be willing to be a missionary, if that is what God wants for me."

Gary breathed an audible sigh of relief. "That's all I ask. That's enough."

# Rejoicing in Hope

# Rejoicing in Hope

## Chapter 14

The following day North Texas was surprised by an unexpected snowfall of an inch. The schools were closed for Christmas vacation and, of course, the children were joyfully making snowmen. Cecily tried to remember when was the last time she had seen snow in December, and was forced to admit that she might have seen it in Texas once or twice before in her lifetime. Freezing rain was another matter. That was not unusual for Texas in January.

Cecily had stayed home with her aunt, ostensibly to help her complete preparations for the family Christmas celebration. If her color was higher than usual it could be attributed to the warmer-than-usual room temperature. Her heart beat in anticipation of Gary's arrival from Michigan.

The day dragged on slowly, because she expected news about Gary's arrival momentarily, although the daylight hours were actually short. When the gray skies darkened early, Cecily began to give up hope that Gary would be arriving in DFW Airport that day.

Mary was sitting in the living room, reading a letter she had just received from Rachel Kruyter. She looked up and noticed the despondent look on her niece's face.

"No word from Gary yet? I imagine that 'standby' tickets won't be that easy to come by this close to Christmas. I just received a letter from Rachel. Would you like to read it?"

Cecily was tempted to say no. She wanted to hear from Gary, not from Rachel, but she decided it would be too rude to say so, so she asked, "Have you finished reading it already?"

# Rejoicing in Hope

"Yes I have." Mary stood up and extended the letter to Cecily. The latter unfolded the sheets and read:

Dear Mary and Jason,

We are all well, thank God. It's Sunday afternoon and Richard just took the children out for a walk to give me some free time. They love to explore the hills with their Daddy.

The last few weeks have been peaceful in the villages. Our translation work continues. We are still struggling to find an adequate term for "Lord" in Guará. The only terms we have discovered so far are kinship terms. If you are not a relative, you can be addressed as *xok ũm*, which is about as polite as saying "you thing." Certainly this is not a term that could substitute for "Lord." There is one other exception: they have adapted a Portuguese term used for a co-sponsor of a Catholic child's christening (*compadre* and *comadre*) by which the Guará address non-Indians whose names they don't know. But as far as the Guará are concerned, there are no social obligations on either side.

Some of the older Guará people have championed the use of *yãyã* (a term of address) and *ũxuxyã* (a term of reference). The latter term now also refers to a livestock owner. In the kinship system, this is the maternal uncle and both grandfathers, who are the opinion leaders in their respective kinship groups or bands. Here we do have definite social obligations, so this is probably the term we will be using for "Lord" in our translation.

# Rejoicing in Hope

The term for "relative" is *xapé*, which is also extended to include people who are not related to them, but who live within the kinship guidelines or rules. This is a friend who acts like a relative. Richard and I are proud to be included among the *xapé*.

We are pretty sure that we have terms we can use for "trust" and "obey." Laura Marie helped to prove the term for "trust" by being afraid to cross a stream of rushing water. The Indians have confirmed our understanding of the expression *ũkuxa yũm* (the heart sits or rests) by explaining that Laura Marie's heart "doesn't rest in the narrow tree trunk at all (*ũkuxa yũm ohnãg mĩpkup kopa*)." This means that she doesn't trust the narrow tree trunk that spans the creek. The Guará believers say that their hearts rest firmly in Jesus (*yũmũg kuxa yũm ka'ok Yeyox kopa*).

My writing time has run out. I can hear the voices of Richard and the kids, so they'll soon be home. I'll tell you more about our discovery of some other Guará words that are key to our translation in my next letter.

Love,

Rachel, for Richard, Laura Marie, Jerry, and Hannah.

Cecily thoughtfully laid the letter down. Then she turned to her aunt and observed, "What a lot of responsibility to find words that will convey the same meanings in another language! I only know English and a little Spanish, but to find a close equivalent of meaning in two unrelated languages must be quite a challenge!"

# Rejoicing in Hope

Mary smiled. "Someone had to do that for us, or we would have no Bible in English. The Kruyters are trying to do for the Guará what Tyndale and Wycliffe did for us."

"And this is what Gary wants to do." Cecily's voice was thoughtful. "He says he wants to live so that his life has eternal value."

"Isn't that what you prayed for, too?" Mary's voice was soft.

"Yes, it's what I want, but it's awfully scary."

Mary reached out to take her niece's hand. "Don't worry whether you'll be able to do what God asks of you. After all, he made you and he loves you. He knows exactly what kind of a life would make you happy and fulfilled. All you have to do is trust him and obey. He'll give you the grace to do it."

*****

Gary phoned home from the DFW Airport at 4 AM on December 24th. Mike drove to the airport to pick him up, while Jean prepared a celebration breakfast at home.

Gary settled into the passenger seat of his father's car and leaned his head back against the headrest.

"I've been on the way here since day before yesterday. That's a long trip. Quite a change from first class travel."

Mike grinned.

"You'd better get used to it. You aren't traveling on an engineer's salary any more."

"True." Gary admitted. "On the other hand, I was able to witness to a lot of people while I waited to be called in all those airports. Maybe that's what the Lord had in mind."

Mike turned his head to look at his son. "It's quite possible that you're right about that."

# Rejoicing in Hope

They rode on in silence for several minutes.

"Have you seen much of Cecily?" Gary's tone was casual.

"No, I haven't, but Paula has spent a lot of time with her. That will be over now, because Kevin is driving up from Houston this afternoon, and Paula will be pretty much wrapped up in him from here on."

"Cecily is still at Mary's house, isn't she?"

"Yes, I understand she'll be staying there until New Year's Day."

*****

Cecily received a telephone call from Paula that morning at 8 AM.

"Cecily? This is Paula. I thought you'd like to know that Gary got in this morning at about 5 AM. Mom hauled me out of bed to greet him when he got here, and then we had a mammoth breakfast (almost a brunch) after Gary got cleaned up. He had been en route since day before yesterday, so he took a shower and changed his clothes before breakfast. He was starved. He's in bed now, trying to catch up on some sleep before he sees you."

Cecily took a deep breath. "Thanks for calling, Paula. I'll wait to hear from him."

# Rejoicing in Hope

# Rejoicing in Hope

## Chapter 15

When Gary phoned Cecily it was 4 PM and the sky was already becoming dark. Cecily was beginning to worry that she was rather low on his list of priorities. She was arguing with herself whether she had any right to feel neglected.

"Cecily? Sorry to have waited so long to call you, but I was dead on my feet and just passed out when my head hit the pillow."

The note of apology in his voice placated her sense of wrong, and she was quick to reassure him: "Paula said that you spent absolutely hours in airports on the way home. You must be exhausted."

"I feel like a new person after that sleep. What I called to ask you is whether I should go to the Nealey house and spend Christmas Eve with you there, or whether I should bring you here so we can spend it with the Ballards?"

Cecily explained the options open to them.

"The Nealeys will be spending this evening with Uncle Jason's family at one of his sisters's homes. But as I understand it, the Ballards and Nealeys will celebrate Christmas with a big dinner tomorrow at the Nealeys. I don't know Uncle Jason's family at all, so maybe we could go to your family this evening, if I wouldn't be intruding."

"Perfect. I know my folks will glad to have us here tonight. I'll be over to pick you up in about half an hour, if that's all right."

Cecily looked up her Aunt Mary to tell her what their plans were. Mary approved, but asked, "Will the Ballards

## Rejoicing in Hope

exchange gifts this evening, or will their gift exchange be on Christmas morning?"

Cecily was stymied. She had not thought of that possible complication.

"I don't know. I didn't put them on my Christmas gift list. What shall I do?"

"Did you buy gifts for Jason's family? Could those gifts be given to the Ballards instead?"

"I bought a basket of goodies for Uncle Jason's relatives. I suppose I could change the card and give it to the Ballards instead."

"I think that would be fine. Do you have an extra gift card? I have some here, it you need one."

The doorbell rang, and Mary urged her niece to answer the door. Cecily opened it, and found herself enveloped in a hug from a leather jacket. Holding her close in his arms, Gary pressed his lips to hers, and whispered, "I missed you so much, darling."

To Cecily, it was the fulfillment of her fondest dreams.

*****

The family festivities absorbed them until the day after Christmas. On the 26$^{th}$ they joined the shopping crowd with Kevin and Paula to see what was still available and was now at a reduced price. Cecily had received a Christmas check from her parents that she was able to spend. The four young people ate lunch at the Mall's food court.

After they finished their meal, Kevin turned to Gary and said, "When are you two planning to be married?"

Paula caught her breath, and said, "They aren't even engaged yet, are you?" She turned to her brother.

# Rejoicing in Hope

Cecily hastily sneaked a look at Gary's face, and saw that it had reddened. She tried to think of something she could say to relieve Gary's embarrassment, but nothing came to her mind. She averted her eyes, and waited for Gary to respond.

"We haven't got to the point of making definite plans yet. There are too many unknowns and we haven't had enough time together to work out the details."

Apparently Gary's answer satisfied the curiosity of his sister's fiancé, and Cecily drew a breath of relief. She determined, however, to call Gary's attention to his own words as soon as they should have enough time alone to work things out.

*****

Two days later Jason and Mary were in the den, enjoying a video together while Gary and Cecily sat a love seat before the fire that burned merrily in the Nealey fireplace in the living room. Cecily twisted in Gary's arms to face him, and asked, "What exactly are your plans, Gary?"

"Plans about what?" Gary looked down at her, puzzled.

"You told Kevin that there are too many unknowns," she reminded him. ""What is it we need to know before we can make our plans?"

"Oh, you mean about us, our plans. First of all, are you willing to wait for me? You have another college semester, and then you would need to take the two-year graduate linguistics course in order to qualify as a field linguist-translator. Meanwhile I'm scheduled to take the survival course in Mexico, and will probably take on a temporary field assignment in Brazil, if they will accept me. Will you wait for me, even if it takes three or four years?"

Cecily looked up at him with growing resentment.

# Rejoicing in Hope

"You mean that you would go off to Brazil and leave me to study in the States for three or more years until I have the required background to qualify as a field linguist?" Cecily's tone of voice clearly indicated that she thought this was unreasonable. "Are you willing to wait that long yourself?"

Gary frowned thoughtfully.

"There may be a way around that. I think we do well to wait a year, but four years—no, that's too much. I think that you could apply to the translation mission as a candidate in training after you graduate from college, and we can plan our wedding after you've been accepted. Then maybe I could take on a temporary assignment here while you finish training. How does that sound?"

Cecily drew in her breath in relief. "I think that would be better, don't you?" Then she asked, as an afterthought, "If I were not accepted, would you join without me?"

Gary shrugged his shoulders. "There's no reason why they wouldn't accept you, but we can cross that river when we come to it."

"And in the meantime we write to each other once a month?"

"Once a month?" Gary was startled. "No, of course not. We need to get thoroughly acquainted. We could become engaged and write as often as possible. I may not be able to write you every day during the survival course, but we can send each other regular email messages during most of the times we're apart."

Cecily's eyes shone. "I would love to be engaged to you, Gary, and can we announce it and everything?"

Gary took her into his arms and crushed her to him. "Yes, 'we can announce it and everything.' You can even wear my ring!"

# Rejoicing in Hope

As Cecily threw her arms around his neck, she could feel his heart pounding in his chest, and her own heart beat so fast that she felt short of breath.

"Oh, Gary! I love you so much!"

Gary's voice was hoarse with emotion. He said, "I love you more than I ever thought possible!"

# Rejoicing in Hope

# Rejoicing in Hope

## Chapter 16

Cecily was back on campus and deep in her studies when she received an email message from Gary:

> Dearest,
>
> I've been collecting the equipment I need for the survival course, mostly from army surplus stores. I miss you very much, because I keep thinking how much you would enjoy going through this survival course with me. I remember how Jacob worked seven years for Rachel, and then seven more, and "they seemed like only a few days to him because of his love for her."[1]
>
> I am arranging to drive down to Mexico with some of my classmates, so that will cut down on some of the travel costs. Then we will fly down to the south of Mexico in early February in a mission-owned plane for the training itself.
>
> I understand that you're working part time in the business office to reduce your tuition costs. That's a great idea. It will also keep you out of mischief, so you don't have time to get sidetracked by those handsome students.
>
> Rachel Kruyter is now sending me a copy of her reports on the Guará translation project. I'll send them on to you, because they're so

---

[1] Genesis 29:20b

# Rejoicing in Hope

interesting and help to keep us focused on the task the Lord has called us to do.

Cecily downloaded the message from Rachel which Gary had attached to his message:

Dear Friends,

I'm working on some of Luke's parables now, and yesterday I started to translate the favorite story of the Prodigal Son[1]. The Guará Indians enjoyed it very much, but they took exception to the literal translation of the father's final statement, "He was lost and is found."

"Who lost him?" "Who found him?"

I tried to explain that the father had not really "lost" him, but he didn't know where his son was. He didn't know where he had gone until he came back home again, so he had lost him.

"Then he disappeared (literally 'caused himself to be lost' *yãy xaxokgãhã*), but he came back, so he was not found," they insisted. They prefer the rendering "he ran away, but now he has returned."

Today I worked on the parable of the Unprofitable Servant.[2] The whole story is anachronistic in our own society, as well as in the rural communities where we live. The field worker who comes out of the field for his noon meal expects to find it prepared for him. We also think that it is appropriate to

---

[1] Luke 15
[2] Luke 17

# Rejoicing in Hope

express appreciation for a job well done. To say, "Cook some food for me, and when I'm finished eating you can sit down and eat" would go over like the proverbial "lead balloon." An outsider (*ãyuhuk*) man might say that to a woman (his wife, daughter, or a maid), but certainly not to a male employee! Jesus says that the employer (slave owner of his day) would never say "thank you" for a job well done. He would simply expect his worker to do a good job of what he was told to do. The Guará do not express appreciation because they have no word for "thank you." We've tried to substitute an expression like "You are very good. It's enough."

Cecily tried to imagine a society in which no one ever said "thank you." *How would you say grace at the table? And you certainly couldn't have a Thanksgiving feast! On the other hand, having a God-is-very-good feast would be a great idea.*

\*\*\*\*\*

In the final week of January Cecily received a surprise visit from Gary. She knew that he was scheduled to leave for Mexico the first week of February, and had not dared to hope that he would be able to visit her before he left on his survival trip. He further surprised her by slipping a ring on her finger. She had already decided that he would not be able to afford an engagement ring, so she was doubly thrilled.

"Oh Gary! It's beautiful!" Her eyes filled with tears.

\*\*\*\*\*

After Gary left she received several email messages from him while he was traveling south. After a few days they ceased, and Cecily knew that he was out of telephone range

# Rejoicing in Hope

in the wilds of the Chiapas jungle. She prayed for him earnestly and began to pray for herself as well, that she would be a qualified partner for Gary in the translation task.

*****

Cecily had not realized how much the regular communication with Gary by email meant to her, until the messages ceased to come in. She turned to her roommate, but this girl was absorbed in her boyfriend who took up all the time she did not need for her studies. Cecily felt lonely, and on impulse, she telephoned her father:

"Hi Daddy! How is everything with you?"

"Cecily? Well, glad to hear from you. Are you in need of funds?"

"Oh no, I was just missing you, and wondered how you were."

"I'm fine, thanks. Your stepmother and I are packing for a South American cruise, so everything is topsy-turvy here."

Cecily was stunned.

"How long will the two of you be gone? I didn't even know you were planning anything like that."

Randy Senior laughed.

"I think it's been something like three months since we heard from you, so that's why you weren't told. What's new with you? How's your boyfriend Gary? Are you still dating?"

"Actually we're engaged, and I'm wearing his ring."

There was a moment of silence on the telephone line, then:

"Are you serious? You're engaged to be married and didn't even tell your father? What are your wedding plans, if

# Rejoicing in Hope

a father may ask such a nosy question? Were you planning to elope?"

Cecily denied this emphatically. "Of course not, but we aren't sure when we can be married. Gary's taking a jungle survival course right now, and he won't be back for two more months. Then we need to decide whether I should undergo candidate procedures right away or wait until I finish the linguistics requirements."

There was a longer pause on Randy Senior's side, and then he said, "What are you candidating for? I think we need to talk. Can you make it home this weekend?"

"Not really. I'm scheduled to work on Saturday. Can you come here?"

"I'll see what I can do. I'll be in touch."

Cecily heard a click as her father hung up.

\*\*\*\*\*

Cecily felt ashamed. She had seen little of her father in recent months, but that fact alone did not excuse keeping him in the dark about her plans. She was of age, and did not need his permission to marry or make any career changes, but she loved him and was reluctant to cause him pain. She could not expect him to be pleased with her plans for a missionary career, but he was a wise man. *Surely he knows he can trust Gary to take care of me.*

She was in a subdued mood as she made her way to the meeting of the Intervarsity Christian Fellowship. She quietly took her place in the group that was gathering to participate in a Bible study led by a visiting theological student. The Fellowship's leader introduced a tall, powerfully-built young man as Benson Clarke. Cecily could not but admire his dark curly hair and friendly smile. The group had invited him to present his studies on the Old Testament tabernacle, and he

# Rejoicing in Hope

had accepted the invitation as a fulfillment of a Christian service requirement at the seminary.

The Intervarsity group was impressed with the study and its presenter. After the study they invited him to join them in the cafeteria for a further discussion on the topic. Cecily accompanied the group to some tables near the windows and listened attentively while her colleagues debated the relevance of the tabernacle to the theology of redemption in the New Testament. She was so absorbed in the discussion that she was unaware of the attention Benson Clarke was paying to her.

After they finished their lunch, Benson Clarke approached Cecily.

"You haven't said very much, but you certainly haven't missed anything. What is your name?"

Cecily was taken aback.

"My name? Cecily Spears. I think the study is fascinating. It's all new to me."

Benson smiled. "I couldn't agree with you more. What is your major?"

"My major? Business administration. They don't teach us much about the tabernacle in our business courses." She laughed.

He laughed, too. "What are your career goals?"

"Actually, I think I am headed toward Bible translation. My fiancé is in Southern Mexico, involved in a jungle survival course. I'll probably take graduate courses in linguistics after I graduate from here."

Benson's face turned serious. "Are you sure that's what the Lord has in mind for you?"

# Rejoicing in Hope

"Not exactly sure. My fiancé is sure and I want to go where he goes."

Cecily's colleagues were impatiently waiting to talk to their guest speaker, so he turned to her, "Let's get together and talk about this some time. It's important to be sure about where God is leading you."

Cecily was reluctant. She agreed, but only because she wanted to close the subject. She didn't want to scrutinize her doubts any more closely than she needed to.

Cecily returned to her room in a disgruntled mood. *I've asked God to make me willing to be willing to serve him on the mission field. Isn't that enough? What else do I need to do?*

She found a message on her telephone from her father. He was coming to talk with her late Saturday afternoon. *What can I tell him? Why is everyone trying to make me doubt whether I should become a missionary? I wish Gary were here!*

# Rejoicing in Hope

Rejoicing in Hope

# Chapter 17

Saturday Cecily arrived home from work to find her father waiting for her in the dormitory lounge. She greeted him with a hug as he stood up from the recliner chair.

"Hi, Dad! Glad to see you, but sorry you had to come all the way out here to see me."

Randy Senior smiled.

"I had to check up on you. After all, you're planning to add someone to the family, and I need to know what it's all about."

Cecily pulled up a chair to sit closer to her father, but he forestalled her.

"Let's go somewhere and have supper, and then we'll talk," he suggested.

Cecily concurred silently, and they walked out to the parking lot where he had parked his car.

After they had finished their supper, they lingered over cups of coffee.

"So you are actually engaged to this Gary?"

The abruptness of the question staggered Cecily.

"Yes. We've decided everything except when. It sort of depends on what the translation mission decides."

"So you have already applied to the mission and been accepted?"

"Not exactly. I have only been accepted as an approved candidate, not as a full member yet. I won't be eligible for that until after I take the linguistics courses."

# Rejoicing in Hope

"But why do you want to take the linguistics courses? How do they match up with your business administration degree?"

"Gary wants to do Bible translation, and he's excited about going overseas to work with a minority people. I want to be with Gary and share in his work. I guess that's the long and the short of it."

Randy Senior was silent for a long moment.

"It's probably enough for now, but will it be enough after you live in the jungle and try to raise your kids far from all the amenities you're used to? You need a stronger motive than being with Gary to find fulfillment in that kind of a lifestyle. After the honeymoon excitement wears off, you may find that you haven't enough motivation to keep going."

Tears came to Cecily's eyes. She knew her father was trying to stop her from making a big mistake that would ruin her life.

"I want my life to be worthwhile, to count for something. Is that motive strong enough to help me face jungle living?"

Her father regarded her thoughtfully. "It may be. The problem is that we won't know whether that motive is enough until after you're locked into that lifestyle. You're the sweetest daughter any man ever had, and it would break my heart if you were made miserable by some reckless life choices. I would like to get to know Gary a little better before I decide he would be a good choice for you. I know he visited us at Thanksgiving, but that was when your grandma died, and I was tied up with making decisions about her burial and funeral."

He took her hand, and beseeched, "Will you promise not to be in a hurry about making decisions as drastic as joining a mission and marrying Gary? Give yourself time to be sure

# Rejoicing in Hope

what would be right for you. Allow me time to get acquainted with your young man."

His anxiety moved Cecily, and she promised she would not make a reckless decision about marriage or about a missionary career.

*****

The following Monday evening Cecily received a phone call from Benson Clarke, the Bible study teacher for the Intervarsity Bible Club. He reminded her of the study of the Old Testament tabernacle that would be held the following evening, and asked, "May I have some time to talk with you after the meeting?"

Cecily hesitated.

"I guess so, but it can't be for long, because I work after school and need evenings to prepare my class assignments."

"I promise I won't keep you over an hour. Will that do?"

Cecily said, "Maybe thirty to forty-five minutes would be better. I need that time to do my reading in the library."

"Agreed." Benson hung up the telephone, and left Cecily wishing she had simply refused to meet with him. *He's going to try to talk me out of becoming a missionary, I'll bet. Why is everyone trying to discourage me?*

On Tuesday evening they met in a secluded corner of the library and conversed in subdued tones. Benson began, "First, let me say that I know God will bless you for your willingness to follow him to the ends of the earth."

Cecily looked at him in surprise. She had not expected him to express so strong an approval of her motives.

He continued, "Having said that, I do want to point out that the flaw in evangelizing a minority people is that they have virtually no influence in the society at large. It would

## Rejoicing in Hope

be much better to evangelize people who are in a position of power among the people. One example is evangelizing university students who have a potential of influencing their society.

"Americans sometimes do more harm than good in trying to influence the poor minority peoples to accept the gospel. One reason is that the Americans' affluent lifestyle confuses the poor and raises false hopes of attaining a similar lifestyle when they accept the gospel.

"Another reason is that Americans are very aggressive in pressing their message on the people, some of whom only 'accept' the gospel because they don't want to offend the foreign missionary.

"A third reason is that Americans tend to be flamboyant foreigners who usually fail to understand the traditional leadership structures and lack the patience to enlist these leaders in any project they may propose. The consequence is destructive to the social organization of the people and results in demoralization. What often happens is that westernization substitutes for Christianization and a syncretistic form of Christianity emerges."

Benson paused, and Cecily asked, "Are Europeans better missionaries than Americans? If so, why?"

Benson shook his head.

"The best missionaries are those from within the minority societies themselves. They understand their own language and culture the way no foreigner ever can. The best mission strategy is probably to train someone from the minority group and send him back to evangelize his own people."

Cecily saw some flaws in this missionary philosophy.

# Rejoicing in Hope

"How can we enlist someone from the minority group to become a missionary? Someone from the outside needs to bring them the gospel in the first place, so that they can hear God's offer, see their need of salvation. Only after they have been evangelized themselves can they see the need to evangelize their own people, right?"

Benson frowned. "My point is that Americans are too rich and aggressive to make good missionaries. It would be better to finance Christians from the third world and enable them to go to the minority peoples."

Cecily rose and excused herself.

"Thanks for explaining your missionary strategy to me. I don't think we should send people from the third world to do what we would be reluctant to do ourselves: leave our wealth behind and spend whatever time is needed to learn from the minority people by living among them."

She heard Benson begin to sputter, but she smiled at him and said, "Sorry, I have to go. It's getting late."

As she hurried back to her dorm, she wished she could discuss this with Gary. *Gary is planning to go the an isolated tribe in the Xingú River valley, to live among them and learn their language so that he can share the gospel with them. I don't know what high tech equipment he plans to take with him, but it wouldn't be much. I wonder what Rachel Kruyter would say about Benson's missionary philosophy. Maybe I should write and ask her.*

# Rejoicing in Hope

# Rejoicing in Hope

## Chapter 18

Late Wednesday evening Cecily downloaded a computer message from her Aunt Mary. Mary had attached a copy of Rachel Kruyter's message, which read as follows:

Dear Jason and Mary,

Let me tell you about the Guará secrecy. It took a long time to win the people's confidence. The need for secrecy is so deeply ingrained that any question gets the automatic response, "Ĩntu, 'a' yũmmũg 'ah (I don't know)." You can almost see their mental computers running the questions through their programmed systems: 1) Who may be angry if I tell? 2) What may be some unpleasant after-effects if I tell? 3) What kind of answer are they hoping for? 4) Will they be annoyed if I give another answer? 5) Do I care?

When I need any information I have to go from one person to another, total the answers up, and average them out. Then I have a base from which to elicit more reliable information.

In the early days I was desperate for words. I would get a word from one Indian, and test it on another. Indian #2 would ask, "Who taught you that word?"

"John Doe (Indian #1) did."

"Well, John Doe knows it. I don't. Ask him." Period. No more discussion. No one is

## Rejoicing in Hope

going to get himself into trouble over a silly thing like a word. Blood has flowed for less reason than being publicly contradicted!

So now, when I test a fact or an expression, I do it this way:

"Is this good talk, is this how the *tikmũ'ũn* (Guará) talk? 'Mary took up (gave birth to) Jesus in a cow house?'"

"Who said that? Who told you that?"

"*Tikmũ'ũn* (the people) did."

"Ah-h-h!" Evident relief. "Yes, that is how the Guará talk. That is good talk."

The cause for the relief is probably two-fold. First of all, he does not know who he is confirming or contradicting. Secondly, since I haven't given my source away to him, he probably won't be betrayed to the next person. Now he is free to give additional information, and probably will, especially if no one is around.

Just how reliable is any Guará-elicited information?

That depends on how you got it.

When someone comes and volunteers information, however private and sensitive it may be, it is nearly always reliable. But if you elicited this information by direct questioning, watch out! Indirect questions are much better, especially if the person thus trapped is left a way to beg off. If he hesitates a bit before answering, don't close in on him. Better yet, back off. Any answer he gives under pressure

## Rejoicing in Hope

just isn't worth it, and demoralizes both of you. It shames him before his peers, and you can't depend on his word under those conditions. Your mutual trust and respect is worth much more than a bit of information, however much you would like to have it.

Cecily put the message down, and smiled. *Someone like Rachel is worth a dozen ordinary missionaries. Surely she's as competent as any missionary from the Third World. She has been able to leave her technological superiority behind and can learn from the minority people among whom she is living.*

Cecily knelt beside her bed and lifted her heart to the Lord:

*Lord, am I doing the right thing to study linguistics and to apply to the translation mission? I know that I can't marry Gary if I am unwilling to leave my comforts and go to live in an Indian village with him. Please prepare my heart to leave all these comforts behind to bring your Word to one of these isolated people groups. I want to serve you, even if I have to give up Gary to do it. Show me, Lord, what you want me to do!*

\*\*\*\*\*

In the days that followed, Cecily felt a lightness in her heart. As the spring semester drew to a close she prepared for graduation. She graduated *magna cum laude* and sang in the college chorus. She invited her father, her stepmother, her Aunt Mary, and her Uncle Jason to her baccalaureate service and her graduation. Mike and Jean Ballard represented their son in the reception that followed. Gary was not due to return home from Southern Mexico until the following week, and so he missed her graduation. The weeks during which she did not hear from him seemed like months

# Rejoicing in Hope

to her, and she was reassured when Jean Ballard would phone to ask her whether she had heard from Gary, because his family had heard nothing from him, either.

Cecily had already enrolled in the Graduate Linguistics School for the course beginning in mid-July. Meanwhile she would stay with the Nealeys until early July, when she planned to return to her father's home with Gary for a week. During these weeks she helped out in her Uncle Jason's office and took care of her cousin Jay so that his mother could work on her lesson preparations for the literacy course, which dealt with the principles and methods of teaching people (primarily adults) to read.

*****

Cecily waited to find time alone with her Aunt Mary to discuss the issue of Americans as missionaries. She achieved this the week following her graduation while she was awaiting news of Gary's return home.

"Aunt Mary, you were a foreign missionary. In your opinion, do Americans make good missionaries or not?"

Mary was mending some clothes and looked up from her work. "What is this about?"

"The Bible teacher at our Intervarsity meetings said that Americans don't make good missionaries, because they are too pushy and their standard of living is far above that of the people they are trying to reach. What do you think about this?"

Mary looked thoughtful. "Some Americans are very effective as missionaries, and others are not. But the same could be said of any nationality involved in missionary work. It isn't a question of national orientation but of ability to love, to put someone else's needs before your own. I believe that when the Lord calls someone, he offers to qualify them for the task to which he calls them."

## Rejoicing in Hope

"Then you believe that when a missionary fails it may be because he was never called to that life in the first place? Or could it be that he or she did not look to God to qualify them for the work?" Cecily wondered if it was really that simple. Mary backed off.

"Maybe. It's possible that they were never actually called. Who knows? Or maybe they were unable to put the people's interests before their own."

Cecily resolved to discuss this with Gary when he returned. He could come home any time now. The days dragged by slowly while she waited for his return in an aura of unreality.

*****

In the second week following her graduation she received a long distance call from Gary. He was phoning from Mexico City, telling her his travel plans. The connection was poor, with a lot of static.

"Cecily, I'm on a reserved flight to Chicago and will transfer in O'Hare Airport to a flight headed for Dallas-Fort Worth. Do you think you can meet me at the airport?"

"Absolutely. When will you be arriving in DFW?"

"I should be arriving on Wednesday at 2 PM. It seems as though I've been gone a year already. How is everybody and everything there?"

"We're all fine. Just waiting for you to come back. Would you like me to notify your family that you're coming?" Cecily offered.

There was a burst of static, then she heard: "Sure, if you would. That would be great." Gary hung up.

# Rejoicing in Hope

# Rejoicing in Hope

## Chapter 19

Cecily notified Gary's father and mother of the time of their son's arrival. Mike telephoned shortly before the flight's estimated arrival time to apologize for his inability to meet the flight. He explained that he was dealing with a crucial problem at his construction site and would not be able to make an airport run until evening. Jean had arranged for a substitute teacher at Gary's arrival time, so she was able to drive to the airport with Cecily.

The women arrived at the DFW airport in good time and located the carousel where Gary would claim the baggage he had checked in. They waited while a long line of passengers filed into the room to claim their baggage. Only a few suitcases remained on the carousel when Cecily saw Gary loom in the doorway, and rushed to greet him. He was helping an elderly woman by toting her hand-carried baggage for her as she was being pushed in a wheelchair, A couple stepped forward to greet the woman, and Gary turned the carry-on baggage over to them. He looked around for Cecily, and his face lit up as he spotted her and his mother among the flight's welcoming crowd.

The thirteen weeks that Gary spent in southern Mexico had given him a bronzed suntan, and the survival hikes coupled with the plain but wholesome meals trimmed him down. He had never been overweight, but now he was trim and very muscular. Jean drove him home where he was welcomed by his sister Paula, who had a summer job at a local child care center.

# Rejoicing in Hope

When they arrived at the Ballard home, Jean's cell phone rang, and Mike was on the line, eager to welcome his son home.

Jean rushed to the refrigerator and brought out chilled cokes for them all. Gary sighed with pleasure as he enjoyed the beverage with his mother's chocolate chip cookies. Then he excused himself to carry his bags up to his room and unpack some of the mementos he had brought for them all. There was no lack of subject matter to discuss at the dinner table, because they were eager to hear about Gary's survival course.

*****

After dinner Gary suggested to Cecily that he walk her to the Nealey home. It was just over two miles to their house, and Cecily agreed. The sun had set and the heat was quite tolerable. It was a magical June night, with a full moon, and a serenade of chirping crickets, not to mention the cicadas. Cecily was overcome with shyness.

At one well-lit street corner Gary paused to pull a package out of his pocket and presented it to Cecily with: "Congratulations on your graduation!" She accepted the gift with a delighted smile. She tore open the wrappings and found a matching set of pearls: a necklace and a pair of earrings. She put them on with Gary's help, and threw her arms around his neck.

"Thank you so much! This is just what I've wanted for a long time. They are just perfect!"

Gary took her in his arms. "I wish I could give you something better. You're so beautiful," he said. "The most beautiful girl in the world!"

Cecily looked up into his face, now shadowed by the trees, and said softly, "You're all I really want."

# Rejoicing in Hope

They kissed under the Texas oak tree.

After they had walked a few more blocks, Gary turned to her: "What are your plans now that you've finished your business degree?"

Cecily had not expected that question, since she remembered that she and Gary had made their plans before he traveled to Mexico. She stumbled on the uneven sidewalk, and grabbed Gary's arm. He helped to steady her, and said, "Or haven't you made a decision yet?"

"Of course I have! I enrolled in the graduate linguistics course and will begin my first classes the end of July."

"Are you happy with that decision, Cecily? Do you feel sure that the Lord is leading you this way?"

"I'm almost sure. I'm not totally sure, but I've asked the Lord to show me, and I'm just taking the first step. I asked him to show me if this isn't the way I'm supposed to serve him."

Gary felt a lump in his throat. "I honestly think this is what the Lord wants for both of us. I think you'll be happy doing this. Bible translation is a service that involves every part of us, everything we are and have. But all during my survival training I kept thinking how much you would enjoy it, how much you have to offer, and I decided that I don't want to go to the field until you're able and ready to go with me. I miss you too much."

Cecily stood still and looked up at him. "I missed you, too. I prayed for you every night and dreamed of the time we can be together."

He kissed her and they were clinging to each other, when Cecily pulled away, overcome by the thought of what a tremendous task they were facing as Bible translators.

# Rejoicing in Hope

"Gary, do you really think we can do this? Do you think we have what it takes to learn and analyze a language, teach a people to read, and translate the Bible for them? Do you think we can show people how much God loves them by the way we live among them?"

Gary took her hands in his. "No, not on our own, but our sufficiency is of God. He called us and he'll enable us."

Cecily remembered her aunt's words, "when God calls, he also enables." She also remembered Benson's warning about Americans being unfitted for missionary service because they were "too pushy" and "too wealthy."

"Do you think other nationalities are more suited to missions than Americans? Does the high standard of living most Americans enjoy make them unsuited for missionary work?"

Gary was silent for a few minutes.

"It could. Particularly if the American in question insisted on maintaining the same high standard of living on the mission field that he had at home. It could raise barriers between himself and the poor people he was serving and provoke them to envy. We need to be sensitive to the people's needs and feelings."

"Are Americans too pushy?

Gary thought about this. "True, Americans are quite aggressive and this may not always be a good thing. On the other hand, that very aggressiveness makes them more willing to involve themselves in missionary work. Certainly most of the missionary force has come from the more aggressive cultures. No culture is perfect, and all missionaries are flawed. We need to recognize our shortcomings and try to keep them under control."

Cecily struggled with the lump in her throat.

# Rejoicing in Hope

"Gary, I worry that I won't be suited for missionary work. I'm not outgoing enough. I'm too shy. I can't imagine myself moving into a situation and taking charge."

Gary smiled in spite of himself.

"Probably that's just as well. We have lots we need to learn from the people before we can try to teach them. But there will be situations when we'll have to take over from them. It's too early to worry about that now, however."

"What do you plan to do this summer, Gary? Will you be asking for an assignment to Brazil in the next few months?"

Gary stood still and took her into his arms.

"I'm asking for a home assignment until you're ready to go. That probably won't be until two years from now. We'll need to do what they call 'partnership development' to raise our support. I think we should get married sometime next fall, and adjust to each other before we try to adapt to other countries and cultures. What do you think?"

Cecily threw her arms around his neck and lifted her lips to his.

# Rejoicing in Hope

# Rejoicing in Hope

## Chapter 20

The week spent at her father's home had its own stresses. Her father was unreconciled to the idea of his daughter being a missionary, and tried to dissuade her from choosing that lifestyle. He had nothing against Gary, he insisted, except for the fact that this young man was determined to immerse himself (and his wife) in a South American jungle. He addressed Gary directly:

"What's wrong with America, that you can't be content to live here? And not satisfied with living in a jungle yourself, why must you impose this harsh lifestyle on your wife?"

Cecily could see that Gary was taken aback by her father's charge.

"Daddy, it's not the lifestyle that attracts us, but we want to bring the gospel to people who have never heard of God's love before. To do that, we need to learn their language, and that requires that we live among them because we can't learn it anywhere else. Some of these languages have never been written down. We've had the gospel for hundreds of years, but they've never heard it yet. We want to bring them the same good news that Jesus ordered us to bring to the entire world."[1]

Randy Senior lost his patience. He continued speaking to Gary: "Look, I don't see why you should take my daughter into a jungle full of tropical diseases because of what someone said two thousand years ago. It may make sense to *your* parents, but it doesn't to me." He stood up and stalked out of the room.

---

[1] Matthew 28:19, 20; Mark 16:15, 16; Luke 24:46, 47

# Rejoicing in Hope

Cecily was stunned. She had known her father would not be in favor of their plans, but she had not expected him to show such an emotional opposition to them.

Gary took her hand and pulled her toward him. Cecily was shaken and her hand trembled in his. Tears sprang to her eyes.

Susan entered the room and asked, "What happened? Why is your father so upset, Cecily?" She glared at her stepdaughter.

Cecily was fighting back her tears, so Gary answered for her, "He's upset that we plan to live in a Brazilian jungle in order to contact a tribe of Indians there."

"You're kidding, aren't you? Of all the hair-brained ideas! No wonder he's upset. After all the money he's put into her education, you plan to do something like that."

Cecily dried her eyes. She had not expected her stepmother to understand their plans, so was not hurt by her intolerance. It was different with her father. He had always been sympathetic to her dreams and aspirations. She knew he would not understand them, but she had expected him to be more tolerant of her ideals.

Gary tugged at her hand and suggested that they visit the mall for a few hours. Cecily agreed silently, and picked up her sweater to wrap around her shoulders.

*****

Gary and Cecily walked through the mall with their hands clasped. As Cecily calmed down, they sat in some lounge chairs that were lined up in the long hallways. Gary pulled out a printout of one of Rachel Kruyter's messages to Cecily's Aunt Mary and passed it over to Cecily. She read:

Dear Jason and Mary:

# Rejoicing in Hope

I've been studying the kinship system of the Guará people. When translating the Bible, it's necessary to know what the Guará terms are for the various relatives. The Guará kinship system seems to be what anthropologists define as an Iroquois system with skewing in the terms of the cross cousins. Let me give you an example:

When I asked Maria what her father's name is, she answered, counting the names off on her fingers: "José, Paxix, Capaonça, and *Capitão* Miguel."

I wasn't prepared for a list of names, since they don't go in for first, middle, and last names. I said, "Which one is your father?"

Now *she* was looking bewildered. "They are all my father group."

I learned that in the Guará system, your father's brothers are also classified as your fathers, and they all consider you their child. Their children are your brothers and sisters. The same holds for your mother's sisters. They are classified as your mothers, and their children are your brothers and sisters. Anthropologists call these relatives your "parallel" relatives. Sexual relations with a parallel relative are considered incestuous.

Your mother's brothers and your father's sisters are more distantly related to you. They are classified by the same terms as both sets of grandparents. These are "cross" relatives, and a male will choose his mate among his

# Rejoicing in Hope

mother's brother's daughters, to whom he does not consider himself to be related (*puknõg*). A woman ideally marries her father's sister's son, to whom she does not consider herself related. A man's father's sister's daughter is called by the same term as her mother and grandmother. Normally a man does not marry this cross cousin who he calls *xukux* (aunt or grandmother). A woman does not marry her mother's brother's son. He is her *ũptix* (grandson or nephew).

If you want to see how this system works out, try to fit your relatives into these categories. It's quite interesting!

Cecily laughed in spite of her heartache, and said, "I think I would need to work that out with some flesh and blood examples! For example, this would mean I would call Aunt Mary my 'mother,' because she was my mother's sister."

"How about your uncles on your father's side of the family? Do you have any?"

"Yes, Daddy has a brother, but they're not close. He lives in California. I can't imagine calling Uncle Bob 'Daddy'!"

\*\*\*\*\*

The rest of the week passed by without incident. They did not mention their plans again, and Randy senior did not bring it up, either.

Cecily began her linguistics course in July, and Gary began his "partnership development" trips about the same time. If Cecily had supposed that she would be seeing Gary every day now that she lived in Cedar Hill, she was doomed to disappointment. She did get to see him daily during the

## Rejoicing in Hope

week they had spent at her father's home, but thereafter speaking assignments kept Gary traveling most of the fall. He was, after all, a single man, young and supposedly appealing to youth groups in the area. But even though he was away much of the fall, they kept in touch by e-mail. *What did people do to communicate before the era of e-mail? Long distance telephone calls are expensive and letters are too slow.*

At the end of the year Gary was home for almost a month, because most churches reserved that period for special Christmas programming. Cecily enjoyed a mid-semester break at the same time. They took advantage of this break to research Brazil's climate, government, and social organization together.

In January Gary resumed his travels and Cecily started her second semester of linguistic studies.

In early February Cecily received an e-mail message from Benson Clarke. He wrote that he planned to be in Dallas that coming week, and asked whether she would be free to see him. She answered by telling him her class schedule and he in turn gave her the precise times when he expected to be in the city.

*I wonder what he wants to see me about,* she thought. *Maybe I'm just the only person he knows in Dallas. I should introduce him to some of my classmates so that he'll be more comfortable.*

*****

When Benson Clarke appeared at the door of her aunt's home, Cecily invited him into her aunt's cozy living room and introduced him to her relatives. After they were seated, Cecily expected him to explain the purpose of his visit, but he was silent. To fill the awkward pause, Cecily asked him whether he was continuing his studies at the seminary in

# Rejoicing in Hope

Texarkana. When he replied in the affirmative, another awkward silence ensued. Mary and Cecily exchanged puzzled glances. Mary politely offered her guest some refreshment, and when he accepted, she left the room to prepare it.

"Are you visiting friends here in Dallas?" Cecily's question was a random shot in the dark.

"Actually, yes. I came to see you."

"You did? That's great. Are you enjoying your studies as much this year as you did last year?" *Why would he come to see me? We have never really been friends.* She decided to leave the choice of conversation topics to him, and sat quietly waiting for his explanation.

After a few minutes of uneasy silence, he began: "Are *you* enjoying your studies? I gather that you are now studying linguistics, right?"

"In general, I think I'm enjoying my courses more than I expected to. It's a lot of work, but at the same time I'm discovering an awful lot about languages in general. I'm also learning a lot about the Lord's ways in dealing with people and I'm getting to know people with very different backgrounds from my own. That's fascinating, too."

Benson looked puzzled. "How does that help prepare you for missionary work?"

"The ability to adjust and adapt to different cultures is very necessary for a cross-cultural missionary."

"But why would you want to adapt to a non-Christian culture? They need to adapt to ours, since ours is a Christian culture."

It was Cicely's turned to look puzzled. "You're kidding, aren't you? Are you suggesting that if we live by the

# Rejoicing in Hope

standards of the American culture we're fulfilling God's standards in the Bible?"

At this moment she was interrupted by the entrance of her aunt with refreshments for their guest. While they enjoyed the soda pop and cake, Benson talked about his part time service in a church that was without a pastor.

As they finished their snack, Cecily stood up. Benson reluctantly joined her, rising to his feet, and she extended her hand to him.

"Thanks for the visit. It was great to see you again, but now I need to get back to my studies because I have a paper that's due tomorrow."

Mary quietly slipped out of the room, carrying the empty dishes to the kitchen. Benson asked, "When can I see you again?"

Puzzled, Cecily thought, *Why does he want to see me again? Doesn't he know I'm engaged to Gary?* She tried to gather her thoughts together. *How can I answer him in a way that he'll understand, but won't be impolite?*

"I don't think that's a good idea. For one, I keep pretty busy with studies and helping my uncle in the office. For another, I'm engaged to Gary, and I'm afraid people would misunderstand it if I spend time with you while Gary is away."

"Why is this Gary so important? How well do you really know him?"

Benson's voice was rough and Cecily didn't know how to answer him. She struggled to put her thoughts into words: "Gary is important because I love him. I admire him very much and want to spend my life with him. He is putting God first in his life, and I want him to be first in my life, too."

# Rejoicing in Hope

"I know, but I think you need to be sure that you have God's mind about this. I just want you to be sure." Benson backed down and his voice became a plea as he took her hands into his own: "Is this is really what God wants for you? I don't believe that this kind of missionary life is what's best for you. I love you, and I want what is best for you."

After he left Cecily went up to her room and knelt by the side of her bed.

"God," she prayed, "please don't let me make a serious mistake, but show me what you want me to do. I just can't seem to be sure about anything these days. What should I do? I think Benson is serious about me, so I don't want to hurt him, but is he right about your will for my life? Is Daddy right about that, too?"

# Rejoicing in Hope

## Chapter 21

During the days that followed Cecily struggled with doubts and ambivalence. *I love Gary, but will his love, as mixed as it is with his sense of calling, be enough for me in the years to come? Is Daddy right about it not being enough to guarantee a happy marriage?*

When Gary returned home in April from a series of speaking engagements, he noted Cecily was troubled. When her anxiety did not diminish with his homecoming, he began to probe to discover the source of her worry.

"What's the trouble, Cecily? Let's talk about it."

Cecily started, and denied having any worries. Gary persisted, "Something is bothering you. Can you tell me what's wrong?"

"It's just that…. It's just that I need to be sure of God's leading for my life. How can I know for sure what God wants me to do?" Cecily struggled to explain the doubts that tormented her.

Gary stared at her. *How can she not know, after all this time?*

"What brought this on, Sweetheart? What happened that you're doubting that God is leading us to marriage and the mission field?" When she did not answer immediately; he said, "Let's talk this over with the pastor. Or is there someone else you would prefer to counsel with?"

Cecily had no one else to recommend, so Gary decided to set up an appointment with the pastor. That gentleman had no time available for the next two weeks, so Gary deferred it indefinitely.

# Rejoicing in Hope

Cecily sensed that Gary was disappointed in her, and this caused a strain in their relationship. She could see that Gary was uneasy about her continued concern as to God's will for her life. In the week that followed Gary tried in every way possible to reassure her of his love. One evening they were returning from a visit to Gary's sister Carol, when Cecily turned to him as he was driving home and asked him, "Suppose we were married and working in the Xingú region and I got cancer or some other serious disease so that I had to go home for treatment. Would you continue to work in the Xingú and send me back to the States? Would you be sorry that you had married me?"

Gary was shocked at the question.

"What do you mean? How do I know what I would do? How can I answer what I would do if something or other happened? It hasn't happened so no such decision is required of me. Why do you ask?"

"I just wonder whether you love me as much as you do the translation work. What would you do if you had to choose between the Work and me?"

Gary showed his frustration

"What are you talking about? That's like asking whether I love my sister more than I do my country. The love I have for you is very different from my love for the work of Bible translation."

Cecily was silent. She still did not know which he would choose if he could not have both. His failure to answer felt like a slap in the face. She touched her engagement ring and fought the urge to cry.

*****

During the days that followed Cecily avoided Gary when she could. This was not difficult, because she had daily

# Rejoicing in Hope

linguistic classes and the evenings were taken up with class assignments. Gary understood this, yet he was hurt that she was too busy to spend time with him. After several days he joined her in the library where she was studying, and simply moved an empty chair close to her and sat down. Cecily paid little attention at first, absorbed as she was in her studies, but after several minutes she glanced in his direction and started.

"Gary!" she whispered. "What are you doing here?"

"I came to see my girl who is too busy to talk to me."

Cecily's face brightened.

"What did you want to see me about?"

"We need to talk. I need to know what is going on in your life, and what you're worrying about." Gary's voice was a barely audible whisper.

"Give me another thirty minutes and I'll be finished with this assignment. Will that do?"

"Sure." Gary looked at his watch, and then got up and browsed through the books on the library shelves while Cecily returned to her studies. She peeked at him, and wondered why she felt so happy now.

It was almost an hour before she closed her books and put her notebook and pens in her backpack. She stood up and searched for Gary among the rows of shelves. He looked up as she approached and smiled. He took her backpack from her and they left the library.

They walked to the parking lot and Gary loaded Cecily's backpack into her trunk.

"Are you hungry? Let's meet at Denny's where we can talk."

"Sounds great." Cecily was unsure whether she was feeling more relief or apprehension.

# Rejoicing in Hope

They met in the parking lot at Denny's. The restaurant was quite full, but the waiting line to be seated was short and they soon found themselves in a booth.

After they were served, Cecily shyly ventured to ask him what he wanted to talk about.

Gary looked surprised. "I sense that you're insecure about our future. Your Aunt Mary told me that you had a visit from someone you knew in Texarkana, and that you have not been yourself since that visit. Can you tell me what it's all about?"

Cecily hesitated. *How can I explain Benson Clarke and why his opinions are important to me? Why should they be, anyway, when he's not really important to me?*

"The visitor you mentioned was Benson Clarke who was the Bible teacher for our Intervarsity group. He taught some great lessons on the Old Testament tabernacle. One day he asked me what I planned to do after I graduated, and I told him that I planned to prepare to serve the Lord as a Bible translator. He seemed to be impressed, and asked for some time so we could talk about my plans. When we got together he discouraged me from missionary work, saying that Americans aren't suited for this because they're too aggressive, and because their high standard of living confuses the people, leading them to believe that accepting the gospel would make them as affluent as the American missionaries. He also believes that we shouldn't adapt ourselves to the culture of a pagan people, but they should adapt to ours, because our culture is Christian."

Gary seized on the final statement and exclaimed, "But what nonsense is this, Cecily! Surely you don't think that our culture is Christian, do you?"

Cecily smiled. "Of course not. And you answered the other questions the last time you were here. But he is so sincere, and I don't know how to answer him so that he understands."

"But none of this explains why you should be concerned about his opinions on missionary work. He's not the only one with the opinions you mentioned, and no doubt many other people have said similar things to you. Why is this Clarke's opinion so important to you?"

Cecily groped for an answer that would be both credible and true.

"I'm not sure, but I think it's partly because he's a sincere Christian and has dedicated his own life to the Lord."

"For cross-cultural ministry?"

Cecily shook her head. "I don't think he envisions that kind of ministry. He seems to think that people from other cultures and languages should learn English and adapt to our culture."

"And what do you think?" Gary probed.

"I think that unless we learn a people's language and culture we can never be sure that they understand exactly what the gospel is about. And unless we're very fluent in their language we may not be using the right words to tell them what God's Word says." Cecily felt frustrated, and was sure that she was not making a lot of sense.

Gary nodded. "There are a lot of pitfalls, I know, but since few people are motivated to learn a foreign language in order to understand the gospel, we still need to learn theirs to show them what God offers in his Word."

Cecily was impatient. "I understand all that, but I'm still wondering where I fit in your list of priorities. I understand that God has to come first, but if you had to choose between me and your work, what would you do?"

# Rejoicing in Hope

Gary frowned. "That's one of the decisions that I hope we never have to make. But one thing I promise you: it's a decision that we would make together. Not just me, nor just you. We would decide that prayerfully, together."

Cecily was not completely satisfied with his response. "If for some reason I couldn't stay on the field, but you could, would you send me home alone?"

Gary sighed.

"Look, Sweetheart, that's like asking me if I would leave my leg behind if it got infected. I could ask the same question of you. Would you leave me if I couldn't carry on as usual?"

Cecily thought about her own parents, who had divorced because of her mother's addictions and chronic infidelity. She argued, "Nobody marries with the idea that they would divorce if they were disappointed. Everyone expects to live happily ever after. But people don't. Not even Christians or missionaries. Daddy thinks that our difficult living situation and the health risks involved will get in the way of being happily married."

The wrinkles on Gary's forehead smoothed out. *Cecily is right. Living in an Indian village is likely to create a situation in which we'll be predisposed to tropical diseases. I don't know what the solution is. I know that the Lord is able to sustain us. The mortality rate used to be higher for missionary wives than for their husbands. She'll have to be very committed to the vision of translating the Bible for one of these tribes, or it would be too hard for her.*

Gary drew her into his arms.

"You're wise to want to make sure. I don't think that living happily ever after is automatic for anyone. We need to give it all we've got."

# Rejoicing in Hope

## Chapter 22

After this meeting with Gary, Cecily decided to get Rachel Kruyter's advice on the special stresses of a missionary marriage. She sent her an e-mail message:

Dear Rachel:

You must be surprised to hear from me, but I am getting lots of advice on missionary marriages from people who aren't missionaries. Since that advice is mostly "don't do it," I need a word of wisdom from someone who did it. That's why I decided to write you: because you are one person I know who actually did it.

My father was quite upset to learn that Gary and I are planning to move to Brazil after we marry, to live with an Indian tribe in the Xingu Valley. He is afraid that our marriage will disintegrate under such primitive living conditions.

Another friend, who was a teacher in our Intervarsity Bible study group, also advises against going to live in an Indian village. He thinks that Americans are poor missionary material, and that we ought to leave that kind of work to people from the Third World nations.

I am personally worrying about where I would fit on Gary's list of priorities. Will the work always come first? Will I be able to face it if he uses me as a handy convenience to

# Rejoicing in Hope

take care of subsistence needs, like cooking over an open fire, washing clothes in the river, etc., while he concentrates on the Indians and their language?

What is your opinion on this?

Love,

Cecily

She had not long to wait. In two days she received a long message from Rachel as an e-mail attachment.

Dear Cecily:

I received your message and can appreciate the dilemma you are facing. It looks as though this will need to be a long message. Please be patient with me as I try to explain how I see your dilemma.

I was never in the same situation as you are. When I met Richard I had already spent a year with the Guará Indians, and one of the first things that attracted me to him was his interest in the tribe. The year I had spent with the Guará exposed me to most of the positive as well as the negative features of translation work. I had faced the dangers as well as the rewards of seeing the first Guará people turn to Christ.

Having said that, let me say that nothing bonds two people together like sharing the same goals. And when you also share the same values and similar backgrounds it becomes a joy to work together. My first partner—your Aunt Mary—and I shared the same goals, but we had different values and different backgrounds. We split up after that year together.

When you are engaged and also when you are newlyweds, you are absorbed in each other. That absorption doesn't last. Gary can't fill all your needs any more than you can fill all his needs. It puts too heavy a burden on a marriage when we expect more from it than what God designed it to do. This is true in any marriage, even where the bread winner needs to concentrate on earning enough for the family to live on, and the homemaker is preoccupied with providing a refuge for her family and rearing children.

Sometimes a marriage is disrupted because one or both parties are immature. Typical of the immature person is the focus on "me, me, me." A mature couple is able to focus on the welfare of the family as a whole and can put some of their personal needs on hold.

My advice to you is to try to make Gary's goals your own, and share your goals with him in turn. There are few joys to compare with the joy of hearing someone's first prayer to the Lord, and watching God transform people's lives. How blest you are to be called to such a ministry!

I strongly recommend that you get some first-hand experience in living in a primitive situation. I expect you will have a vacation due shortly. How would it be if you flew down to Brazil and spent a month or two living with us among the Guará people? You

# Rejoicing in Hope

could help us in lots of ways, and practice learning and analyzing an unwritten language. You won't need a lot of funds for this. You would be our guest for the time you are with us. You only need your round trip airfare and money for bus fare in Brazil. Please consider doing this. Believe me, you will be glad you did.

Love in Jesus,

Rachel

Cecily read the message through, and then read it over again. *What a fantastic idea! That would be one way to find out if I could handle it and if I could be useful in this kind of ministry!*

She knelt by her bed and dedicated her life to the Lord all over again.

Then she began to wonder. *Why did Rachel and my Aunt Mary split up after a year with the Guará? They are such warm friends. How did that happen?*

*****

In the days that followed Cecily checked her calendar and looked into the cost of airfares. Gary was gone again on a series of out-of-state speaking engagements at colleges and seminaries, and Cecily sent her father a message with the information she had gathered in researching the travel channels on the internet.

Dear Daddy,

A friend invited me to visit her family in Brazil over my vacation period. She is a Bible translator who is married and has three children. I would like to see for myself what it would be like to live in a remote area under

## Rejoicing in Hope

primitive conditions, but I don't have quite enough money for the round trip ticket. Do you think you can help me out with the funds I need? I would appreciate it very much.

    Love,

    Cecily

She received a telephone message from her father that very evening.

"Honey, I think going to Brazil to check things out is a great idea, but you'll need more money than just your air fair. Hotels are expensive. Don't get yourself in a corner by underestimating the costs of your trip. If you will tell me exactly where you plan to go, I can plan your trip for you with the travel agency our firm uses. They can handle things like any visas you need, and any airline connections, but you have to get your own passport.

"You don't mention whether Gary is going with you, or whether you will be traveling alone.

"By the way, how well do you know this 'friend' who invited you? Be sure you give me all the information you can about where she lives, etc. If you should run into problems there, it will help me bail you out."

Cecily promised to give her father full information, and then sent a message to Gary:

> Rachel Kruyter invited me to come and spend a month with them among the Guará Indians. Daddy is handling the matter of airfare, tourist visa, and traveler's checks for me. I am getting a passport, which I will need for the visa. My vacation will be from mid-June to mid-July, and I am all excited about going.

# Rejoicing in Hope

I wish you could go with me!

Love,

Cecily

Two days later Cecily received an e-mail message from Gary:

Sweetheart,

You have literally swept me off my feet. I think it's fantastic that you are able to visit an ongoing field project, let alone one in which the Kruyters are working! How I wish I could go with you! I am committed to presenting the translation work until September. I don't see how I can get out of these commitments. I'll check and see if I can postpone some of them. If I can't, please, do me a favor and keep a journal of your experiences so I can at least get a feel for what you are experiencing.

How did this come about? Did Rachel invite you out of a clear blue sky, or did you write to her first? Do write and tell me everything. I expect to come home for a few weeks before you leave, so the time won't move so slowly.

Love always,

Gary

Cecily had never traveled out of the United States except for a class trip to a border Mexican town—Nuevo Laredo—across the border from Laredo in Texas. Since it was a tourist place, it was not altogether typical of Mexico. She was scared to travel internationally all on her own, but Rachel promised to meet her flight in the interior of Brazil, and her Aunt Mary promised to teach her how to pass

## Rejoicing in Hope

through Brazilian immigration and customs. She applied for a passport and received it in due time. Then she sent it to her father who would apply for a tourist visa to Brazil, and waited for it to be granted. Meanwhile she kept up with her classes, began packing her bags, and helped her Aunt Mary by taking over some household chores so that Mary would have enough time to prepare for her upcoming literacy course.

One day she reread Rachel's first message to her and noticed that Rachel's partnership with her Aunt Mary had broken up due to some unexplained incompatibility. *I thought they were such warm friends. I certainly never saw any sign of strain when the Kruyters stayed with us last June. Why did their partnership break up? I think I'd like to ask Aunt Mary about that sometime.*

However Cecily felt awkward about broaching the subject with her aunt, so she put it off.

Gary was able to postpone a few of his speaking engagements, but he could only be in Brazil for two weeks, during the middle of Cecily's stay. Since she was scheduled to stay in Brazil for a month, it didn't seem as though that would be an appropriate time for Gary to join her. Cecily would still have to travel to Brazil and back by herself, which she admitted she dreaded.

*****

Gary shared his discomfort with Mary. She listened to him with a sympathetic ear, but then she said, "It might be a good idea for Cecily to find out that she can handle international travel on her own. She may have to do quite of bit of that after you're married."

Gary protested. "But she's so young. It's a jungle out there and what could she do if she should run into trouble?"

## Rejoicing in Hope

"What would you do if you ran into trouble? Could you teach her how to handle some kinds of trouble she could meet?"

Gary stared at her. "I wouldn't know how to do that, because I don't know what kinds of problems she could run into in South America. I suppose you would be in a better position to do that than I."

"I'll do what I can, but we need to pray and to entrust her into God's care."

During the remainder of that semester Cecily fluctuated between apprehension and anticipation. She had no illusions about being brave, but neither did she enjoy being afraid. If a little thing like traveling overseas was going to "rock her boat," she wasn't fit to serve the Lord anywhere, except maybe right at home.

# Rejoicing in Hope

## Chapter 23

Two weeks before Cecily was scheduled to leave for Brazil she received an urgent call from her brother Randy Junior.

"Cecily, I'm in sort of a quandary here. I need some money urgently. Can you lend me some?"

Cecily was mute with shock. Then she protested, "But Randy, how much money do you need? I put everything that I've saved so far (which isn't much) into traveler's checks for my trip to Brazil. And why do you need money? I thought Daddy paid the tuition that the study grants didn't cover."

Randy Junior sighed.

"Well, that's true. But the money I need isn't for school. It's for something else, and I need it right away. The credit card interest goes up fast."

"What have you been buying on your credit card? If it's books you need, I'm sure Daddy would help you out. Why don't you ask him?"

Randy was impatient. "I told you it wasn't for school. It's just that I took a trip to Europe during spring break with some guys and put the expenses on my credit card. I hoped to get some tuition grant funds that would help me pay for it. I won't get the grant check for another month, but I need money to pay my credit card debt now, and I need cash for my tuition, room, and board. I'm up a creek. Never mind the advice. Just tell me how much you can lend me."

# Rejoicing in Hope

"I'm sorry, but I don't have any to spare. I've been working during vacations to pay my own tuition and part time during the school year to pay for my expenses."

A long silence ensued. Cecily could hear the click as Randy hung up, and she was assaulted by feelings of guilt that she could not help her brother out of his dilemma.

*Why can't he ask Daddy for the money? Susan always liked him better than me; maybe she could bail him out. Would Uncle Jason help? I don't want to be the one to ask him. I wonder how much money Randy owes?*

*****

Cecily sent an e-mail message to Randy Junior several days later, to ask him if he had found a solution to his problem. She received no answer, so the following week she called him long-distance. He seemed to be in a hurry and reluctant to talk to his sister.

"Don't worry about it. I'll find a way somehow. I need to hang up now."

Cecily slowly hung up the receiver. She called him again several days later.

"Have you solved your debt problem yet, Randy?"

"I'm working on it. I'll be OK. Don't worry. Just have a good time on your trip."

The time for her trip was only a week away and she was busy with final exams and helping her Aunt Mary with preparations for her literacy course. *I wish I knew what Randy is doing to cover his credit card debt. Oh, well, I can't help him, so I'll have to let it go.*

*****

The week of finals was a stressful one for Cecily. She averaged about four or five hours of sleep a night, and felt

## Rejoicing in Hope

like a zombie. Gary phoned her the evening before her flight and assured her of his love and prayers for her. She had a hard time making coherent responses because of her fatigue, but the knowledge of his love warmed her heart.

*****

When she embraced her Uncle Jason and Aunt Mary at the ramp to the airline departure gate, she tried to tell them how grateful she was for all their prayers and support. Jason only smiled, but Mary assured her of her continued prayers for safety and wellbeing. Gripping her hand-carried baggage, Cecily turned around and climbed the ramp, pausing at the top to wave to her relatives.

Her trip to São Paulo, Brazil was uneventful, and she slept most of the way. She passed through customs and immigration without a hitch, and boarded the flight to Minas Gerais. She was greeted by Rachel Kruyter at the baggage carousel in Belo Horizonte.

Rachel helped her retrieve her stowed-on baggage, and led her to the parking lot where Richard Kruyter awaited them with the three children. Cecily looked around at the sun-bathed airport with wonder in her heart.

Maybe it was because she was still sleep-deprived, or maybe it was just because her senses were assaulted by all the new sights, sensations, and sounds, but Cecily felt she was in a daze. They stopped for lunch at a restaurant where the food was weighed and priced on the basis of the weight. Richard and Rachel were busy helping the three children to choose the foods to put on their plates, so Cecily was left to pick and choose her own food. She had exchanged some dollars at a São Paulo money-changers booth, so she was able to fumble the correct Real[1] money out of her wallet—with the cashier's help—to pay for her plate of food.

---

[1] Brazilian monetary unit

## Rejoicing in Hope

They traveled on a paved road as far as Governador Valadares that first day, and stopped at an inn with the placard *Rio-Bahia* prominently displayed. The inn had a restaurant, and Cecily helped feed the Kruyter children. Apparently the meal was included in the bill, because no money changed hands here. The menu was boiled beef, some boiled chicken legs, brown beans, rice, and a coarsely ground white root called *farinha*. The children obviously enjoyed the food very much.

Cecily slept in the same room as the two older children. The beds were narrow and the mattresses were hard, but except for a few hungry mosquitoes, they were not disturbed.

In the morning they got up and had a breakfast of thick, strong coffee with boiled milk, tiny loaves of French bread, and butter. After this meal Richard went out to buy bottled water for the trip.

It was a hot day of travel on dusty, unpaved roads, but by late afternoon they arrived at the access town where the Kruyters lived in a rented house. As soon as the Kruyter jeep entered the town, the streets filled with small urchins who were barefooted and wore only ragged shirts or dresses. Cecily felt awkward and strange, but Rachel and Richard accepted the situation as a matter of course. The Kruyter children greeted some of the urchins with the obvious pleasure of greeting friends. Cecily helped Richard and Rachel to unload her baggage from the jeep and carry it into the house.

From the outside, the house looked very much like the neighboring adobe brick homes in the town, but once inside, Cecily saw that Rachel had added some of her own touches to the Kruyter home. There was a small refrigerator and a gas stove with an attached tank of bottled gas. The floors were covered with earthenware tiles, and there were tiles on the roof, but no ceilings over the rooms. Cheerful cotton

## Rejoicing in Hope

print curtains covered the windows. Cecily peeked into the bedrooms and saw that all the beds were covered with mosquito netting. There was a well behind the house, about thirty feet from the outhouse.

Cecily was relieved to find that she had a small room to herself, just off the children's bedroom. There was some kind of an addition to the other side of the house, which Cecily discovered was a study room for language analysis and translation. Richard and Rachel's bedroom was on that side of the house, adjacent to the study room.

After the baggage was brought to the appropriate rooms, Rachel called her family together, and explained to Cecily, "We'll be eating at the *pensão* (inn) tonight and *fazer feira* (shop) at the open market tomorrow morning to stock the kitchen."

They locked the doors and windows and headed for the inn, which was located several blocks away. The adults had to stoop to enter the low doorway. The sun had gone down and the room inside was illuminated only by small kerosene lamps. It took a few minutes for their eyes to adapt to the darkness, and meanwhile the woman who supervised the kitchen brought in bowls of steaming hot food, which she filled from pans cooking on the wood-burning stove in the adjoining, lean-to kitchen.

Cecily was surprised to discover she was very hungry. She helped dish up the food for the children, and then all bowed their heads to ask God's blessing on the meal.

Cecily was puzzled by the local people. She noticed that they were varying shades of dark, and that most had black curly hair, although the adult women wore drab kerchiefs around their heads so it was not possible to be sure of their hair color and texture. When the women had brought in the serving bowls and poured water into the glasses they left for

## Rejoicing in Hope

the kitchen, and she took advantage of their absence to ask Rachel, "Which of these people are Indians? They all look so much alike."

Rachel looked up, puzzled. "You mean these people, here?"

"Why yes. Which of them are Indians?"

"None of these people are Indians. They are mostly descendants of the African slaves that were brought to Brazil during the colonial period. The Guará Indians don't live in town. They live in small villages on the reservation. Some of them will be coming to town tomorrow, I imagine, buying things on the street market. Especially if they hear that we are back."

Cecily heaved a breath of relief. She was glad that they were not Indians, because they didn't look anything like she had imagined an Indian would look.

*****

When they returned to the Kruyter's adobe house, Cecily found she was too tired to do anything but sleep. Rachel smiled at her and said, "Why don't you just unpack something to wear tomorrow and then crawl into bed. I'll show you how to tuck in your mosquito net so the insects won't bother you during the night."

# Rejoicing in Hope

## Chapter 24

Cecily woke up in the morning to the sound of the roosters crowing. She soon learned that the idea that roosters crowed to greet the dawn was a myth. The roosters crowed at intervals all night long.

She crawled out of bed and out from the mosquito net that had protected her all night. *Funny how safe that mosquito net made me feel!* She donned her jeans and a shirt, and then noticed that it was humid and chilly. She pulled out a jacket to wear over her tee shirt.

She could not hear anyone else stirring in the house so she tiptoed to the window in the main room and opened the shutters. The fog was dense outside, but she could hear that the townspeople were stirring. She also heard pigs squealing. According to her watch it was six in the morning. She returned to her bedroom and opened its shuttered window to enable her to see, and began to unpack her suitcases. There were not enough hangers to hang up her clothes, so she doubled them up, several articles of clothing to a single hanger. By the time she had stored her clothes in the wardrobe it was light enough to read her Bible.

Laura Marie called her for breakfast, and she found the table set with the thick coffee, boiled milk, little French breads, and butter. This was to be the standard breakfast menu during her entire stay.

As the family finished breakfast, Rachel turned to Cecily.

# Rejoicing in Hope

"I'm going to the square to buy some groceries. Richard will stay with the kids. Do you want to come along with me, or would you rather stay home?"

Cecily said, "I'd like to go."

As they walked toward the town square, Rachel said, "We're planning to drive out to the reservation today to visit the Guará people. Are you feeling up to going along? The kids will stay. We leave them with one of the ladies from the church we attend, and it seems to be working out all right."

Cecily's eyes glowed.

"I'd love to go along, but I won't understand anything they're saying, will I? On the other hand, I don't know any Portuguese either, so it would be the same if I stayed here."

Rachel laughed. "Now you know how Richard felt when we came here together after we were married. I had spent a year with them and had a good working knowledge of the Guará language, but Richard couldn't understand a word. He was one up on you, though. He had studied the national language Portuguese, so he could fall back on that in a pinch."

"Do you think I can do some language learning practice during the month I'm here? Will there be someway to do that?" Cecily realized that it might not be convenient for the Kruyters if she embarked on a serious program of learning the language, but she wanted very much to try.

"We've been counting on you doing just that. You can also try your hand at teaching the people to read their own language. In fact, some of the townspeople might appreciate it if you could help them learn to read Portuguese. Many of the older people never learned to read. The children all go to school and usually finish a few of the lower elementary grades, but lots of the adults never had the chance to study."

# Rejoicing in Hope

"But how can I teach them to read a language that I don't know myself?" Cecily was intimidated by the thought of teaching a language she couldn't speak.

"It won't be easy," Rachel admitted. "but there are ways to accomplish it. However, you only have a month, and we need to use that time to the best advantage for your training and the people's benefit. I think you should probably concentrate on language learning."

When they arrived at the village square where the weekly market was held, Cecily noticed that only staple foods were sold. There were no fresh vegetables or fruits for sale. She saw open sacks of brown beans, of rice in the husk, and coarse salt. There were dark brown-colored bricks that Rachel told her were made from crude sugar cane, called *rapadura*. Packages of finely-ground coffee, and ground manioc flour (*farinha*) were available. She saw fresh and salted, dried meat. Pigs had been butchered at dawn and the fresh pork lay on the tables. Other tables offered salted, dried beef, called *carne do sol*. Black flies swarmed over the meat. There were live chickens for sale, tied together by their legs and hung from a log. Eggs were sold individually, wrapped in cornhusks to protect their delicate shells.

Pitifully thin dogs gathered around the market and tried to grab some of the meat. The vendors repelled them with kicks and sticks. The dogs yelped loudly, adding to the noise of the bustling market.

Cecily noticed that Rachel did not bargain for better prices. When Cecily asked her about it later, Rachel explained than an attempt to do so would have convinced the vendors that she was trying to cheat them. Instead, if she thought the price was too high, she would shake her head regretfully and say she couldn't afford to pay that. Often the vendor would reduce the price. If not, Rachel would thank

## Rejoicing in Hope

him politely and look for the article at another stand, for a lower price.

After Rachel had purchased the necessary food staples, she and Cecily returned home and the family climbed into the jeep for the trip to the reservation. Cecily took a spiral notebook along with her so that she could write down her first impressions of the people and their language. She noticed that both Richard and Rachel took folders along. On the way to the reservation they dropped off the Kruyter children at the home of their *crente* (believer) friends.

Riding in a jeep on unpaved roads is a far cry from traveling in an American-built car on paved highways. The country roads were unpaved, of course, and since the terrain was hilly, the jeep climbed up rutted inclines and dived down through flooded valleys. Cecily was glad she didn't need to take the steering wheel because the road looked precarious in more than one place.

When she was not preoccupied with worrying about the roads, Cecily noticed that they could have been alone in the world, as far as she could see on either side of the road. The trees were scraggly and sparse. At one point they suddenly met a truck coming from the opposite direction around a sharp bend on a steep hill. Cecily gasped, and Richard pulled over to the downward slope of the hill as far as was possible, to let the truck pass them. The truck driver sounded the horn as a "thank you," and continued on his way. Rachel and Cecily got out of the jeep while Richard struggled to get the jeep back on the narrow, slippery road. Then the women climbed back into the vehicle. Richard heaved a deep sigh and wiped the perspiration from his forehead and neck as he continued on his way.

Before long they met a group of people coming from the opposite direction. They looked very different from the townspeople. All the clothes the people wore had a brownish

# Rejoicing in Hope

tint. The women had long, straight black hair, and the men's hair was also straight, but trimmed. The few children who accompanied the group wore only shirts or dresses. The shirts were obviously worn by little boys who wore no pants, and the ragged dresses defined the little girls. The men carried bows and arrows, while the women carried mesh bags on their backs, suspended from their foreheads. The entire group was brown, except for their hair. Their skins were brown, their clothes were brown, and the bows and arrows were brown. Even the mesh bags (woven from tree bark, Cecily learned) were brown. She understood why Rachel had said that the Indians looked very different from the townspeople.

When they approached the headwaters of the creek, Richard stopped to ask a man a question. The man grinned, and answered. Richard got back in the jeep, and said to Rachel, "He says it's shallow enough to cross over at the bend near Severino's house."

When they approached the bend Richard stopped the jeep, and waited for Rachel and Cecily to step down. Then he drove carefully through the stream and waited for the women on the opposite shore. Rachel and Cecily removed their shoes and socks and prepared to wade across the stream.

Cecily noticed that the water was also brown, and she followed Rachel, stepping gingerly into the stream. She clung to her shoes and socks and waded across the thigh-high stream. She wanted to ask why they couldn't simply have driven across in the jeep with Richard, but decided against it because it sounded too critical. Rachel smiled and answered her friend's unspoken question.

"The soil is so soft in the creek bed that Richard wants to lighten the load. He is afraid that otherwise the jeep might get stuck in the middle of the creek."

## Rejoicing in Hope

Cecily was embarrassed at her own lack of trust, but appreciated Rachel's understanding.

They climbed back into the jeep on the opposite shore and then drove to a village just over the hill and out of sight from the creek. As Richard parked the jeep, the people began to swarm out from the village, and greeted the Kruyters with smiles. The children huddled close to the adults and eyed the newcomer solemnly. Cecily self-consciously smiled at them, while they continued to stare wide-eyed. Then one child stepped forward, grabbed Cecily's tee shirt, tugged at it, and said, "*Ã' hõm topixxax!*"

Not understanding the Guará language, Cecily helplessly turned to Rachel, who smiled and said, "She just asked you for your shirt. It's best to ignore that and simply smile back at her."

Cecily looked down at her shirt in baffled unbelief. *Did that child really expect her to strip off her shirt here in public?* With relief she took Rachel's advice, and turned to look at the other villagers surrounding them. She saw that some of the adults were looking at her, laughing, and talking to each other, so she supposed that she was the subject under discussion. *Why not? They probably don't see strange foreigners around here that often.*

Richard was talking to the few men who had been in the village, and the women were talking with Rachel. Relieved to be ignored for the time being, Cecily looked around at the tiny huts in the village. They were built in a semi-circle, with a packed-mud area in the center of the village. There was one wattle and daub hut (mud plastered over a log frame) and the other huts were made of thatch, both walls and roofs. Some huts had walls all the way around, but others had only two or three walls. It was a pleasant day, and blackened clay pots—covered with banana leaves—were cooking on the ground, on a hub of five smoldering logs shaped like spokes on a

## Rejoicing in Hope

wheel. Several huts had doors to bar entrance to the hut, but others were open.

Cecily was shocked back to the present when Rachel spoke to her in English:

"Adela is willing to come to town to teach you her language. She'll come mornings and will leave for home after lunch. I'll take care of any arrangements about paying her. She'll come tomorrow, so that will leave you this afternoon and evening to prepare for the lessons. She has never taught anyone her language, so it will be up to you to set up the lessons ahead of time. Have you had the language learning course yet? If so, you'll have a pretty clear idea of how to go about planning your lessons."

Cecily gulped. "Okay. I'll work on that today."

While Rachel visited families where a member had been sick, Cecily tried to recall her lessons. How she wished she had brought her Language Learning lesson outlines with her! She would just have to do the best she could.

# Rejoicing in Hope

# Rejoicing in Hope

## Chapter 25

Back in the access town that afternoon, Cecily kept busy preparing for the language learning session with Adela she would have the next morning. She gathered natural objects together in order to elicit terms that were familiar to the Guará people, such as sticks of various sizes, and pebbles, also varied in size. She wrote down words for body parts, resolved to hunt up samples of straight human hairs and curly human hairs. She picked out brown beans (for singular and plural), worried about how to elicit contrast of gender (if this existed in the language), adjectives (long, short; wide, narrow; pretty, ugly; light, dark; young, old; male, female; etc. Then she wrote down action words (verbs): jump, walk, run, sit, lie down, talk, sing, hoe in the garden, cook food, sleep, get up, etc. She arranged them all in her spiral notebook, knowing that unless she was prepared, she would forget most of these in the morning under the tension of eliciting the words.

Based on the elicited terms, she would begin to analyze the speech sounds. She knew that the Kruyters had already done a phonological analysis, but working out her own analysis would help her to learn the language.

While she was working on lining up potential meaning distinctions in Guará, a group of teenagers from the access town came to the door. Cecily was taken aback, since she knew no Portuguese at all. She smiled, however, and communicated her linguistic deficit by smiling and shrugging, using her hands to emphasize her lack of understanding. After a few minutes of futile questioning in Portuguese, the teenagers found courage to air some English words they had learned in school. Some words Cecily could not understand at all, but some she tried to guess at. They

## Rejoicing in Hope

were inviting her to participate in something, but she wasn't sure what. Rachel was in her study working on translation, so Cecily did not want to disturb her. She smiled at her young guests and gestured with her hands to show that she could not speak Portuguese. When her guests realized that Cecily could not understand what they wanted, they smiled back and left the house saying, "*Até logo* (goodbye)."

It flashed through Cecily's mind that she would need some key Guará elicitation phrases in order to get the desired results from her language learning lessons in the morning. She realized that she would need to get those Guará phrases from either Richard or Rachel that evening, since the Indians did not know any English. Cecily seized her notebook and wrote down some elicitation phrases she would need from Rachel in order to collect language data from Adela in the morning:

What is this?

What is that?

What are those

What are these?

How many are these?

She would also need comparative terms: larger than, smaller than, taller than, shorter than, harder than, softer than, older than, younger than, lighter than, heavier than, better than, worse than, etc. Not to mention possessive pronouns like mine, yours, his and hers, ours, theirs, and similar expressions.

When Rachel finished with her translation session, Cecily begged her for the basic elicitation forms in the Guará language. Carefully mimicking Rachel's pronunciation, she wrote down the phrases in phonetic script:

*Pute ũm nũhũ?* (What is this?)

# Rejoicing in Hope

*Pute ũm õhõm?* (What is that?)

*Hãpxop xohxix te xĩy?* (How many things are they?)

*Ãxuxet'ax te xĩy?* (What is your name?)

*Ũxuxet'ax te xĩy?* (What is his/her name?)

*Ũkxuxet'ax* Cecily (My name is Cecily.)

*Putep mũn ãte' mĩy?* (What am I doing?

*Putep mũn tute' mĩy?* (What is he/she doing?

Cecily worked hard to memorize the phrases she would use in her first language learning session in the morning.

*****

After their evening meal Cecily washed the dishes out at the well in their back yard. She had considered offering to read stories to the children, but realized that Rachel would probably prefer to have that special time with her children since they had been at their baby sitter's all day.

After the children were settled in bed, Rachel and Richard shared what they had learned in their separate sessions that day. Cecily listened with interest, but did not interrupt them with requests for explanations. It was enough to know that each translation session could involve some new discoveries about the Guará language.

*****

At noon on the following day Cecily reviewed her spiral notebook with its phonetic entries of Guará language data. She struggled to pronounce all the words correctly, and then realized that she needed to prepare for the next day's collection of language data. She could use the words she had collected today to gather fresh language data tomorrow.

# Rejoicing in Hope

While studying her first day's collection she heard Rachel call her name. She stood up and found her way to Rachel's study room where she sat at the computer.

"Did you call me, Rachel?"

"Yes, I did. I was just downloading my e-mail and I find a message from Gary for you. Why don't you sit down here in my chair where you can read it and keyboard your reply." Rachel stood up from the computer to make way for Cecily.

Cecily read:

Dear Rachel,

By now Cecily should be in the access town (at least, so I hope), and I would like to send her a message. Could you please pass this along to her? Thanks.

Dearest,

I have been thinking of you daily, and thanking God that you have the opportunity to get a taste of what real language work is like. I can't wait to hear about it.

I received a phone call from your father yesterday, and he complained he hadn't heard anything from you yet. I told him I hadn't either, and that since you were traveling in the interior I hadn't expected to hear from you yet. By my calculations, however, you should have arrived at the Kruyter's access town by now, so I am hoping to hear from you soon.

Carol is beginning to look like she's carrying twins, but the doctor says not. It just looks like it. She is really bothered by the hot Texas weather.

# Rejoicing in Hope

Paula is busy planning for her wedding. Dad says he's glad he only has two daughters. Three would be too much of an expense. Tell me, are you planning an expensive wedding? I guess the bride gets to choose which kind of wedding she or her family want.

Write soon,

Gary

Cecily settled down in front of Rachel's computer and wrote:

Dear Gary,

I arrived at the Belo Horizonte airport safe and sound two days ago. I was met by all five of the Kruyters and we drove to Governador Valadares in their jeep, where we overnighted. The roads were paved until we reached Teófilo Otôni, and after that it was dusty dirt roads all the way. It had rained quite a bit, so there were some low mud holes to navigate, but we made it fine.

When we arrived at the access town it seemed that the entire childhood population came out to greet us. They lined up in front of the bus stop and stood in complete silence while they watched us. Rachel and Richard were used to it and it didn't faze them a bit. I found it very unpleasant to be stared at silently by so many round, dark eyes. The Kruyter kids seemed to know a lot of them; they waved and greeted them in Portuguese.

Since the larder was bare, we walked over to the inn (called a *pensão*) and had supper there. There was no electricity, so we

# Rejoicing in Hope

ate rice, beans and chicken by kerosene lamp. Afterward we walked home, but I was so tired by then that not much registered with me. Rachel helped me unpack an outfit for the morning, and tucked the mosquito net around my bed for me.

The following day Rachel and I shopped at the open market in the town square. No fruits or vegetables were sold there, only staples and meat. After we returned home with our purchases, Richard and Rachel dropped the kids off at the home of the woman who baby-sits them, and we drove to the reservation to see the Guará Indians.

When I first saw the townspeople I had wondered which of them were Indians and which were not, but Rachel told me that none of them were. When we got to the reservation I saw that the Guará look very different. But my message is becoming too wordy, so I had better not explain any more now.

Yesterday an Indian woman came to help me to learn the Guará language. I had a fun time eliciting words and writing them down in phonetic script. What I learned about the language so far will have to wait until another time.

I miss you. Don't forget to write, and tell Daddy I'll send a message to him next time I have access to Rachel's computer.

Love,

Cecily

*****

# Rejoicing in Hope

In eliciting the names of body parts Cecily had found some discrepancies in her notations. In words that should mean "we" and "our" she got different responses. She held up her hand and said, *ũgyĩm* (my hand), and when she took Adela's hand and held it up next to her own, she was instructed to say *yũmũg yĩm* (our hands). Yet when she took Rachel's hand and held it up next to Adela's, the latter indicated that she should say, "*ũgmũg yĩm* (our hands)."

Cecily had already discovered that the language had no gender distinctions. There was no difference between "he," "she," and "it" in the language, nor between "his," "her," and "its"; but there was a significant difference between the "we" that included the one addressed and the "we" that excluded that person.

When they ate their simple supper of eggs, sweet potatoes, and greens, she mentioned the pronoun distinctions she believed she had discovered. Richard smiled.

"You're doing very well, if you've made that discovery this early in your research. Yes, the language has the first person plural pronouns in both the inclusive and exclusive forms. To say, "*ũgmũg xit*" is to exclude the person who is addressed. It says "we (someone else and I) are going to eat, but not you." But to say, "*yũmũg xit*" means that the person you are talking to is included."

Cecily laughed. "I can see that those pronouns could come in very handy. You have to be careful in translating those pronouns, I bet, since the Greek language doesn't have those distinctions."

Richard nodded. "Other problems occur when the Guará language lacks a word that is important in the Greek. Such as 'to thank.' We need a clearer idea how the Guará people express appreciation."

*****

## Rejoicing in Hope

Cecily enjoyed her biweekly trips to the reservation with Richard and Rachel. As she learned more vocabulary, she was able to converse with the Guará on a limited number of subjects, and enjoyed it very much. The Guará showed their pleasure in her attempts to communicate with them.

One day, in the second week of her stay, her visit coincided with the death of a Guará child. The little girl must have been about six years old, and her wasted body was laid on the sapling bed in the family hut. Cecily was shocked to see how gruesome death is without the cosmetic treatment given corpses in her homeland. The mother was keening, joined by relatives. Cecily turned to Rachel and asked why the child had died. Rachel, with glistening eyes, said that the child had apparently suffered from some kind of food poisoning and did not respond to treatment. In trying to console the mother, Cecily fumbled for words. She wanted to tell the mother that the child was with Jesus, but she not only lacked the vocabulary to communicate this, but she also was not sure what sort of biblical basis she had for this assurance. *Lord,* she prayed, *please comfort her heart. I don't know what to say, and anyway, words are so pitifully inadequate!* Her thoughts turned back to the day when she learned that her own mother had died of a drug overdose. But her mother had apparently seen Jesus as she lay dying, because Aunt Mary said she smiled and uttered his name.

*Dear God, you were so very good to my mother, who surely didn't deserve any of your kindness. Please comfort this Guará mother and the other relatives who are grieving the little girl's death. Comfort them because you want the children to come to you, because you said that the kingdom of heaven belongs to them.*[1]

---

[1] Matthew 19:14

# Rejoicing in Hope

## Chapter 26

In the third week of Cecily's stay with the Kruyter family she witnessed a major Guará tragedy. The villagers had been able to sell their mesh bags and bows and arrows for cash, and promptly traded in the money for cane liquor (*cachaça* in Portuguese, or *kexmuk* in Guará). They bought enough bottles of the alcoholic beverage to carry back to their villages and promote a full-scale binge.

Cecily was working with Adela in the Kruyter home, when her language teacher got up and ran to the open window to identify the sounds coming from the market place. Cecily joined her and could hear the singing and shouting coming from that area. Adela promptly excused herself. She said, "*Ũgmõg* (literally I go: the cultural farewell)," and dashed outside to join her relatives. Cecily was stunned, and moved to follow her into the street, when Rachel called to her, "Don't go, Cecily. There will be trouble out there. Just stay here."

The normally quiet Guará tribespeople were shouting and singing. The townspeople emptied the streets and locked their doors and windows. The only places remaining open were the bars, where the proprietors illegally sold alcoholic beverages to the Indians at exorbitant prices.

Cecily was frightened. Certainly the fear was palpable all around her. "What about the kids? Should we go and get them from the babysitter's house?"

Rachel said, "Richard has already gone to pick them up. What we need to do now is pray. Pray for Richard and the kids, for the townspeople, and for the Guará people. These binges always mean trouble."

## Rejoicing in Hope

Rachel moved to lock the window shutters and the doors. Then she knelt with Cecily to pray for the town and all the people who were in it.

Absorbed as she was in prayer, Cecily only belatedly became aware of banging on the door. She and Rachel rushed to the door simultaneously, and called for the person outside to identify his- or herself. They heard the muffled response:

"It's us, Richard and the kids."

The women slid aside the bolt and opened the door. Richard was carrying little Hannah while Jerry and Laura Marie were clinging to his belt. As soon as they were inside, Rachel slid the bolt back into position.

"Mommy," Jerry's voice trembled, "Something awful is going on out there. People are fighting each other, even the women are pulling each other's hair and rolling over the ground. What's wrong?"

Rachel took him into her arms. "They've been drinking *cachaça* and it makes them wild. They don't even know what they're doing when they're drunk like that."

Laura Marie protested. "They're awful, Mommy. I don't ever want to go back there."

Even through the locked doors and shutters they could hear the distant sounds of pounding and the shattering of glass.

Rachel led the family to the kitchen and dished up the food that had been prepared for their *almoço* (main noon meal). While they were eating they could hear that the sounds of violence were fading into the distance. This meant that the Guará people were returning to the reservation, where they would probably continue to fight until the effect

## Rejoicing in Hope

of the alcohol wore off sometime before the following morning.

The Kruyter children relaxed and ate a good lunch of beans, rice, *farinha*, and eggs. Little Hannah fell asleep in Cecily's lap, and Jerry was nodding in his booster seat. Laura Marie politely excused herself and went into the darkened *sala* to play with her dolls. Richard and Rachel put the younger children down into their beds with a sigh of relief.

Rachel looked at Cecily, and smiled. "I can see you have about a dozen questions stirring in your mind."

Cecily admitted this was true. Rachel looked at her with a question in her eyes. Cecily responded, "The first question is 'why?' Has this traditionally been their cultural expression of frustration, or is this a behavior they learned from the dominant society?"

Richard entered the conversation. "I understand that this is something they learned from the dominant society. That is to say, apparently they had no alcoholic beverages of their own, but the colonists soon discovered they could control the Indians by giving them alcohol. They could seize Guará land and their women when they were drunk. Of course, these binges are a Guará improvement on the original idea. They're community-wide events of blowing their minds. It includes men, women, and children."

"Are there Christians among the Guará? Do they participate in the binge drinking? Did Adela leave because she was scared?" It was hard for Cecily to imagine that the friendly tribespeople could wholeheartedly participate in this violent activity.

"Are you thinking that Adela rushed out of here to find a place of safety? I personally doubt it. I think she was rushing to participate in the excitement with all her relatives. After

## Rejoicing in Hope

they blow off all this steam they are quiet and friendly again. To answer your question, not everyone participates. A few of the people withdraw, but it seems clear that this kind of excitement exerts a strong attraction on most of the Guará people."

"How often do they have these binges? Can you predict when they are likely to occur?"

"We haven't made much of work of predicting them. So far we haven't been too successful in our casual attempts." Richard shook his head.

"What about the Guará children? Is there any hope that they'll stop having these binges when they grow up? I imagine they suffer the most from parental neglect and violence during these episodes."

Rachel agreed. "You'd think so; but once they get to be teenagers they often are more radical than their parents."

Unwilling to accept the idea that the problem had no remedy, Cecily protested: "But Rachel, surely we need to make work of keeping binges out of the Christian church."

Rachel shrugged her shoulders.

"Until they themselves see these binges as evil and destructive, no amount of decrying from our side is likely to be effective in eradicating them. We need the Holy Spirit to show them the destructiveness of this practice. But you're right. We need to keep on teaching them that God wants them to be filled with the Spirit, not with alcoholic beverages."[1]

\*\*\*\*\*

---

[1] Ephesians 5:18

## Rejoicing in Hope

The following morning Cecily was awakened at 7 by a cough at the front door.[1] She listened as Richard's footsteps led to the door, and she heard a dialogue being held in the Guará language. She heard the door being closed cautiously, and Richard's footsteps retreated to his bedroom. She heard Rachel ask him a question, and she heard that he answered, but she could not understand what was said. A few minutes later Rachel rapped on her door, and Cecily invited her in.

"What is it, Rachel?" she asked.

"Adela's husband José just came and asked me to go and see his wife who he says is sick. I wonder, would you stay and take care of the kids? I don't want to delay my visit to the reservation, and so I wondered if you could watch over the kids. Just let them play at home today, OK?"

"Did he say what was wrong with her?"

"No, but that's not unusual, especially if it's a gender-related problem. Richard will drive us there, and I'll see what I can do to help, if anything."

Cecily crawled out of bed while Rachel returned to the kitchen. Shortly afterward Cecily could hear them both talking to their visitor, and then their voices faded away. She heard the door close, and a key turn in the lock. Then she heard the jeep motor start, and the sound faded away as the vehicle pulled away from the house.

Cecily dressed and checked on the kids. All three seemed to be asleep, so she went to the kitchen to prepare breakfast for them. *Lord, I wonder whether Adela got beaten up yesterday in all that violence, or is she just sick from a hangover?*

*****

---

[1] A dry cough is the Guará way of knocking on the door.

# Rejoicing in Hope

It was a long day, and Cecily was challenged trying to find ways of keeping the children busy while they played in the house. The access town was very quiet all day, but it seemed that the usually friendly non-Indian neighbors were avoiding them. Cecily wondered whether they believed the foreigners might be responsible for some of the violence. At least, some probably thought that the foreigners should have been able to stop the destructive behavior.

Cecily took advantage of the break in her study of the Guará language to work on memorizing the vocabulary items she had already elicited from Adela.

When Richard and Rachel had not returned by sundown, Cecily could not deny her fears that they had become victims of the brawling people. She tried to maintain her calm by reading to the children after she had fed them a supper of corn starch pudding. Hannah crawled in her lap and promptly fell asleep there. Jerry sat next to her on the backless bench and leaned against her arm. Laura Marie sat on her other side. When Cecily paused in her reading, Laura Marie asked, "Why aren't Daddy and Mommy home yet?"

Cecily had been asking herself that question for several hours already, but she downplayed her own uneasiness and said, "I suppose they are trying to help Adela, who is sick."

"But it's almost night," Laura Marie protested. "They should be home."

Cecily forced herself to smile, and assume a reassuring tone. "I think what we should do is to pray for all of them. I think that's what God wants us to do now."

Laura Marie nodded, and folded her hands.

"God, please take care of Mommy and Daddy and make Adela well quick."

Cecily's heart echoed an "amen" to this prayer.

# Rejoicing in Hope

*****

It was already 11:15 and the children were sound asleep in their beds. Cecily felt very lonely and cut off from the world. The access town did not have telephone service to the homes, and there was no way that Richard or Rachel could call her to inform her of Adela's condition. She could not even find out whether the Kruyters were safe and well.

*I can understand why they asked me to take care of the kids at home today, after the scare they had in the community yesterday. I also realize why they can't send me word, but I sure feel lonely and scared. I think I'll stay up for a while so that I can hear the kids if they call. I'm afraid I would sleep too soundly to hear them, and that would certainly upset them.*

She decided to check Rachel's computer to see if there was any e-mail for her. At that late hour there was usually sufficient electrical power to run the computer. She had just downloaded a message from Gary and printed it out, when she heard a jeep motor approaching the house. Reluctant to open the window in case it could admit an intruder, she held her breath, as she heard the car door slam. Someone turned a key in the lock, and then the door opened with a slight creak. Richard stepped inside and Cecily caught her breath with relief.

"Richard! I'm so glad you came! Where is Rachel? Have you had any supper?"

Richard slipped off his wet windbreaker and sighed.

"It's been a long day. Rachel stayed in the hospital at Águas Formosas where we took Adela for treatment. Adela doesn't speak any Portuguese, and someone really needs to be with her to explain things to her. Rachel decided to stay and sent me home to check on the kids.

# Rejoicing in Hope

"No, I haven't had any supper. Have you got some leftovers here?"

"As a matter of fact, we do. I'll warm them up for you on the little kerosene pressure stove." She hesitated, then said, "I almost forgot. I just downloaded a message from Gary and haven't turned off the computer and printer yet." She headed for the study room to take care of that matter, when Richard put out his hand and stopped her.

"Why don't you just warm up the supper, and I'll turn off the computer and printer. Then I'll give you a report about Adela."

He turned to the study, and Cecily went to the kitchen to warm up supper for Richard.

# Rejoicing in Hope

## Chapter 27

Cecily waited impatiently for Richard's explanation of what was wrong with Adela, but held back to allow him time to eat first.

Noticing Cecily's anxious expression, Richard began to explain the entire situation.

José had awakened them that morning with the message that Adela was very sick and needed medicine.

"We asked what was wrong, but he sidestepped the question by simply insisting that Rachel go and help his wife. He said Adela was *xok putup* (wanting to or going to die), and said he didn't know what was wrong. Since there was a possibility of some residual violence from the binge, I thought it was better for me to drive Rachel and José to the reservation. The jeep would then be available if we needed to take Adela to the nearest hospital, which is a clinic in the city of Águas Formosas. We didn't want to take the kids to their usual baby sitter because yesterday's violence was still too fresh in their young minds. We really appreciate your willingness to help us out and to provide the kids with some security.

"When we got to the village where Adela lives there was almost no one up and about. Most were still sleeping it off, and some were hurt from yesterday's fights. Other people were sick from the inferior quality *cachaça* (sugar cane alcohol) they had imbibed yesterday. We went straight to José's hut and found Adela bruised and smelling foul from the results of yesterday's binge. When we asked José who had beaten her up, he mumbled that he didn't know. And it may be true. He may have done it, or anyone else, for that matter.

"Adela did not respond and Rachel did a superficial physical examination. Her heartbeat was fast and irregular, her blood pressure was high, and she seemed to be unconscious. Rachel was concerned about her, and thought we should bring her to the nearest hospital, because there might be internal injuries. She had difficulty getting José's permission, and Adela's mother (who lives in the same domestic unit) objected loudly. It was only when Rachel promised that she would stay with her until one of her family could come to take care of her, that her family consented.

"We loaded her into the jeep and took José along. Adela's mother wanted to go with us, but our jeep could not transport more than four people with Adela taking up the entire back seat. Beside, we knew that the clinic personnel would would be unhappy if they had to cope with drunk Indians.

"I stopped at the reservation's office on our way to town to inform the agent what we doing. The man in charge came out to the jeep to look Adela over, tried to question her husband, and then dismissed us. Of course, the Indian Agency will be billed for her care, and that will probably be a hassle, but the agent only remarked that he could not promise to reimburse us for the gasoline we used to transport her.

"We found that the clinic staff was not happy to accept an Indian as a patient. We had expected no less, but they did receive her, albeit reluctantly, after they heard that Rachel would stay with her overnight and could translate for the staff."

Richard paused to warm up a cup of cold coffee.

# Rejoicing in Hope

"What did the clinic doctor say about her condition?" Cecily asked.

"He said she was suffering from intoxication due to the poor quality alcohol she drank. He merely shrugged when I suggested that she must have been in a fist fight. Rachel will have her hands full when Adela regains consciousness."

Cecily felt enormously relieved that Richard was home to take responsibility for the children. He peeked at them as they lay sleeping, and then turned to Cecily.

"Thanks so much for taking care of them. I'm sorry to do this to you, but the children will feel much safer with you than with their Brazilian *babá* (baby sitter). I'm going to get some sleep now, and in the morning I'll have to go back to the reservation to bring one of Adela's relatives to the clinic and relieve Rachel. We'll see how things go."

Cecily bade him goodnight, and picked up the printout of her e-mail from Gary, which she had not yet read. She retired to her room to read it by flashlight.

> Dear Cecily,
>
> It is really a treat to get such up-to-date news from you instead of having to wait for ten days or two weeks to get a message. You are getting some very practical experience in what a translator's field work involves. I am delighted for you.
>
> When you return in just under two weeks, I hope you will have time to visit some of the churches that have expressed an interest in contributing to our support on the field. Remember to take some pictures of the Guará to bring home with you.

## Rejoicing in Hope

Your Aunt Mary has been under the weather lately. She seems to be lethargic, and so the folks have not been meeting on Sundays as regularly as they used to. She is getting ready to teach her course (she calls it a "mega-literacy" course) at the linguistics institute. It may be the weather that is responsible for her lethargy; it has been hotter than usual this year.

Love,

Gary

Cecily folded up the printout thoughtfully. *I wonder if Gary will be so thrilled to hear my report of the binge and its aftermaths?* She laid the sheet aside and got ready for bed. She knelt at the bedside and prayed, "Lord, show me what I need to learn from the experiences of the last two days. Show me."

*****

Rachel Kruyter came home late the following evening. She had slept very little during her time of attendance on Adela. The nursing care given at the clinic consisted primarily in giving medication. All the rest was done by relatives who attended the patients. There was virtually no night shift staff in the clinic, so even medications—when indicated—had to be given by the relative or friend who attended the patient at night. At first Adela had been comatose and required little help, but as she regained consciousness she became restless and keeping her in bed was quite a struggle. She was frightened by all the strangers around her, and only Rachel seemed able to soothe her as she spoke to her in her own language. Adela did not speak—not even to Rachel—which raised fears that she had suffered some brain damage.

# Rejoicing in Hope

Adela's husband José disappeared during the first night. There had been no word from the Indian agent, and the clinic director was pressuring Rachel to sign for the clinic bill. This she refused to do, knowing that the Indian Foundation was responsible for the medical care of Brazilian Indians, considered wards of the Federal government.

As Cecily entered the final week of her stay with the Kruyters, the children returned to the home of the *babá* and resumed playing with the caretaker's children. Rachel was slow to recover her strength, and Richard admitted some concern for her health.

"She has rheumatic heart disease, and while she does very well as long as she gets enough rest, I have to watch her. She carries a lot of responsibility, you know."

Yes, Cecily did know this. She was glad that Richard was looking after her, because Rachel would be almost impossible to replace in the family or in the translation program. Adela was expected to be discharged the end of that week, but that was too late for Cecily to resume language learning with her. Meanwhile she was happy to help out with the children and domestic chores. She was able to elicit some language data from the occasional Guará visitors who came to the access town to seek medical help, and this encouraged her to continue enriching her Guará vocabulary.

One afternoon during the final week of her stay she accompanied Richard, Rachel, and the children on a visit to Adela's domestic group. Cecily wanted to say goodbye to her language teacher.

She found Adela reclining on her sapling bed, working on weaving a mesh bag. She was very thin, and her eyes were large in her thin face, but she smiled at Cecily.

# Rejoicing in Hope

"*Tep hã?*" she greeted ("What is the purpose of your coming?")

"*Ãhãk nũn,*" Cecily replied (I came for you). "*Ok ãhittup* (Are you well/happy)?"

This launched Adela into what some would call an "organ recital," meaning a recitation of her many ills and symptoms. Cecily listened patiently, but she understood only a small fraction of Adela's complaints. She was relieved to see that Adela's early aphasia (loss of speech) was not a problem any more.

Cecily burned to know what had caused Adela's many bruises, but she realized that she lacked the necessary vocabulary to define those bruises and to understand any explanation that Adela might offer. After all, she might have been too drunk to remember how she received those bruises, anyway.

"*Ũgmõg hãptox ha,*" Cecily explained. "*Yõgnũ pet hak mõg, hãptox hak mõg* (I'm going to my home, I'm going far away)."

Adela's face looked anxious. "*Hãm ũm hã put pu ãnũn* (When are you coming back)?"

Cecily had no plans to return at all. *What do I say now? Maybe just that I don't know.* "*Ĩn tu. Ap yũmmũg 'ah.*"

Adela seemed disappointed. In her face Cecily read doubt: *Why does this foreigner come and try to learn our language, and then go away again?*

\*\*\*\*\*

As Cecily packed her clothes for her return to the United States, she sorted some souvenirs she had acquired. She had a bow and arrows, but Richard warned her that she would not be allowed to carry them on the plane. A better choice would be the mesh bags woven by the women. She also

## Rejoicing in Hope

packed up some copies of Guará primers that Rachel had given her. She found she was eager to get back home to warm showers, to flush toilets, to electric dishwashers, to washing machines and dryers. But she would miss some Guará friends, the Kruyters—both adults and children—and first and foremost, she would carry away the memory of Rachel's gift of herself to the Guará people.

Cecily sent an email message to her father to notify him of her travel plans.

Dear Daddy,

How are you all? I am well. Did you receive the message I wrote you when I first got here?

This has been a very full month, and I wouldn't have missed it for anything. It's another world. While I'm looking forward to going home, I know I will miss the Kruyter family and the Guará Indians more than I can say.

I will be leaving Brazil next week. The Kruyters will take me to the Tancredo Neves Airport in Belo Horizonte. I will fly from BH to Congonhas in São Paulo, and from there to DFW. I won't be able to go to Texarkana for a few weeks, because my classes start two days after I get back. I look forward to seeing you on Labor Day, though. I plan to drive up there for the long weekend. I hope to see you all when I get there. I have lots to tell you.

Thanks so much for everything.

Love,

Cecily

# Rejoicing in Hope

# Rejoicing in Hope

## Chapter 28

It was a rainy day when the Kruyters drove Cecily back to the Belo Horizonte airport. To Cecily, it all seemed like a dream. Had she really spent nearly a month among the Guará Indians? She had her spiral notebooks to remind her of the language lessons and the cultural notes she had taken. When Richard unloaded the passengers and the baggage at the Tancredo Neves International Airport terminal, Cecily threw her arms around Rachel's neck, and said, "Thanks so much for everything, Rachel. I wouldn't have missed this experience for anything. I will never forget you or the Guará Indians."

Rachel returned the hug, and kissed her friend on both cheeks, Brazilian style. "I can never thank you enough for all you did for us during this month you stayed with us. If you ever want to come back, just let us know."

Cecily hugged each of the children individually, and then gave Richard a Brazilian *abraço*.[1] Laura Marie turned sad eyes to Cecily, and said, "Are you coming back soon?"

"I don't think so, but I really don't know. I will soon see your Aunt Mary and I'll tell her I got to meet you. She'll want to know all about you."

"Will you tell her about me, too?" Jerry was feeling left out.

"I certainly will, and she'll want to hear all about you." Cecily turned to give a final kiss to little Hannah, who had been whimpering. Hannah did not take kindly to strange situations, but she responded to Cecily's kiss by throwing her little arms around her neck.

---

[1] Hug, embrace

# Rejoicing in Hope

*****

The trip back to Dallas was uneventful. There had been an unscheduled layover in São Paulo—a delay of an hour caused by the late arrivals of connecting flights. Cecily took advantage of the wait to make a quick visit to the airport's McDonald's. We *Americans may make fun of our hamburger joints, but the burgers taste pretty good after a steady diet of beans and rice.*

When she arrived at DFW International Airport she felt as if she had been away for years. One of the airport guards greeted her with a "welcome home!" and she felt as if she had come home.

In the baggage claim area she met Gary, who had managed to be home to meet her flight. When he took her in his arms, she knew she really was "home."

*****

"I can see you've lost some weight; not that you were ever heavy, but you *are* a bit thinner. Have you been well?"

Gary's question brought her up short. "I've been fine the whole time, but it's been such a busy month that I feel dazed by all that happened. I suppose my steady diet of beans and rice are at least partly responsible for my slight weight loss. If I start telling you about my experiences now, I won't know how to stop before tomorrow sometime."

Gary laughed. "That figures. What I really want to know is whether you're glad you went."

"Oh yes. I wouldn't have missed it for anything. I feel as if I never really lived before I met the Guará Indians. I thank God for granting me that opportunity, and for Rachel who made it possible."

Gary's face glowed.

# Rejoicing in Hope

"Thank God for the opportunity you had of getting this kind of experience first-hand. I want to hear all about it after you're rested."

Gary took her directly to the Nealey home and helped her to unload her baggage. She met her Aunt Mary at the door. Cecily noticed that her aunt was pale and seemed to have lost weight, but her face brightened when she greeted her niece.

"Cecily! We sure missed you. Has the trip been worth it to you?"

Cecily hugged her.

"Very much so. I wouldn't have missed it for the world. I want to tell you all about it, but I'm so tired now that I think I'll need to get some sleep before I start my report."

Mary laughed. "Of course. Let's take your baggage up to your room."

*****

When Cecily woke up it was dark outside. *Have I slept the clock around? I wonder what time it is. I wonder what day it is!*

She turned on the light switch and saw that it was nine o'clock. *It must be 9 PM. I wonder if Aunt Mary and Uncle Jason are still up?* She cautiously opened her door and stumbled slightly on the stairs. There was immediate silence in the den, and Cecily lashed at herself for her clumsiness. She found her uncle and aunt lounging in recliners. She smile and hugged them both.

"I guess I slept off my travel fatigue by now. Has Gary gone home already?"

Aunt Mary smiled. "He didn't stay around very long after you went to bed. We invited him to join us for breakfast

# Rejoicing in Hope

tomorrow morning. What are your plans for tomorrow, by the way?"

"I have to check in at the Graduate Linguistics Institute tomorrow to find out my grades from last semester and to make sure that I'm properly enrolled for the next semester. Then I need to pick up the textbooks and syllabi that I'll need. Classes begin day after tomorrow already."

Mary raised her eyebrows. "Are you hungry enough to want some supper?"

Cecily's smile was sheepish. "I guess so. Was there anything left over from supper?"

"Come and see." Mary slipped her arm under Cecily's elbow and drew her to the kitchen.

*****

When Gary came over for breakfast the following morning, he asked, "When can I have that report you mentioned yesterday?"

"Well...I have several things I have to do this morning, but I should be free for that report by mid-afternoon. I'd kind of like to include Aunt Mary and Uncle Jason in this, because then I wouldn't have to say the same things twice over."

"Fair enough." Gary turned to Mary, and asked, "Will Jason and you be free to hear Cecily's report this afternoon?"

"I'll check with Jason. I'm not sure what his schedule is like today. For my part, that should work out just fine. How about inviting your parents, too, Gary?"

"Good idea." Gary picked up his cell phone and punched in his mother's number. He got a mechanical response, so he tried his father's number. When Mike answered, Gary invited him for Cecily's report. Mike

# Rejoicing in Hope

apparently gave a positive response, so Gary told Mary, "Off hand, it seems this afternoon will work for most of us. If we have it late enough—some time after four—Mom should be able to attend, too."

Jason had a prior commitment, and he asked Gary to tape Cecily's report so he could hear it later.

*****

After Cecily's report to her family it was time to turn her attention to the new semester at the Graduate Linguistics School in which she was enrolled. Gary had to leave for his scheduled meetings, and Cecily became absorbed in her studies.

Cecily had signed up for the Mega-Literacy course which her Aunt Mary taught. It was an interesting course, but, sitting in her seat and watching her aunt as she taught, Cecily noticed that her aunt had lost a lot of weight. She wondered if Mary, always weight conscious because she had a short, stocky build, was deliberately losing weight. Although she was thinner, her abdomen was not. She remembered Gary's comment of some months ago, that her aunt was having some health problems. She determined to ask her about that, whenever it would be convenient.

One evening her Uncle Jason knocked on the door of her room. Cecily was writing an essay on literacy, and called, "Come in."

Jason opened the door, and apologized for interrupting her.

"Sorry to bother you, Cecily, but your Aunt Mary is not feeling well. Do you think you could fix us some supper?"

"Of course. Let me go downstairs and see what we have in the pantry. Tell Aunt Mary not to worry." Cecily saved her work on the computer and stood up.

# Rejoicing in Hope

She looked around in the kitchen and found that her Aunt had prepared potatoes and vegetables for cooking, and that the meatloaf in the refrigerator seemed to be ready for the oven. She prepared the meal, set the table, and when everything was ready, she summoned her uncle and cousin Jay to come to the table. As they came, Cecily asked, "Does Aunt Mary want some supper? Is she coming, or can I take her a tray in her room?"

Jason said, "I don't think she wants anything right now. Just fix her a plate of the food, cover it, and put in into the fridge. She'll probably want some a little later."

After supper Cecily cleaned up in the kitchen while Jason put little Jay to bed. Then she went to her aunt's room and knocked on the door. She heard a response from Mary, and entered.

"I'm sorry you're not feeling well, Aunt Mary. Is there something I can do for you?"

Mary shook her head. "No thanks, Cecily, but I appreciate your asking."

The room was darkened so she could not see very well. There was only one small lamp giving light. Cecily thought her aunt looked pale, but could not be sure.

"We put aside some supper for you. Would you like it now?"

"No, thanks. I haven't eaten anything, and yet I feel stuffed." Then she laughed softly. "For years I struggled with my weight, trying hard not to gain, and now I am losing weight without even trying. One thing is, I'm not hungry. I wish I knew why."

Cecily couldn't help worrying.

"Have you been to a doctor, Aunt Mary? Are you sure that something isn't wrong with your digestion? It isn't

# Rejoicing in Hope

normal for you to be losing weight. You ought to check it out."

Mary said, "Actually, I did go to our family doctor and he checked me out. He said he couldn't find anything wrong with me. He thought it might be part of my 'hormonal change of life.' So this seems to be something that I just have to go through."

Cecily did not know enough about a woman's life cycle to evaluate her aunt's statement. *Maybe she's right. Maybe this is just something like hot flashes, only involving the digestive system.*

"Please let Uncle Jason or me know when you want some supper. If this doesn't clear up within the next few days, I think you should ask your doctor for some medicine to help you feel better. You owe that to Uncle Jason and little Jay."

Mary smiled and thanked her niece. Cecily bent over to kiss her aunt and left the room. She met her Uncle Jason at the foot of the stairs, and he stopped her.

"Is she awake, Cecily? How is she feeling?"

"Yes, she's awake, but I don't think she's feeling very well. She just said she wasn't hungry. I asked her if she wanted supper and she said, 'Not yet.' She says she feels 'stuffed.'"

Jason looked worried. "I took her to our doctor and he says he can't find anything wrong, but it's not like her to take to her bed during the course. I'm afraid something is wrong."

# Rejoicing in Hope

# Rejoicing in Hope

## Chapter 29

The following morning Mary seemed to be more like herself. She fixed breakfast for her husband and son. Cecily was used to fixing her own breakfast, and hurried off to get to her first class on time.

After her classes that day she realized that it was time to get in touch with her father and Randy, Junior, so she sent them an email message:

> Dear Daddy,
>
> It seems a long time since you heard from me. I returned from Brazil just last week and am already immersed in my classes here. Because it's a three-hour drive, I hope to visit you this coming weekend, if that is all right with Susan and you.
>
> How is Randy Junior doing? He said he was in a financial squeeze last month when I left for Brazil. Is he back in college now?
>
> I am very glad I was able to go to Brazil and I thank you from the bottom of my heart for making it possible. It wasn't exactly fun—some of it was downright scary—but I learned an awful lot. I'll tell you about it when I come.
>
> Remember me to Randy and Susan.
>
> Love,
>
> Cecily

Two days later she received an answer from her father.

> Cecily,

# Rejoicing in Hope

I'm glad you enjoyed your trip to Brazil. We are anxious to hear all about it when you come.

Randy got into a mess. Apparently he got himself head over heels in credit card debt and tried to raise the money he needed in illegal ways. Since this is his first offense, he might not get any jail time, but he will certainly be on probation and having this on his record will also hamper his career. I'm trying to raise the money to pay his fine. I'll fill you in on the details when you come.

Love,

Dad

Cecily reread the message, unable to believe her eyes. *How could Randy have done this? He knows better!* Then Cecily felt guilty that she had not been able to help her little brother when he needed her. *Poor Randy! This is something he'll always regret.*

\*\*\*\*\*

Mary returned to her classes and said nothing more about her digestive discomfort. Cecily noticed, however, that while she fixed meals for her family, she partook of very little herself. She caught Uncle Jason looking at his wife with concern. *What is he worrying about? Surely he'll take her to a doctor soon!* She suggested as much to him: "Uncle Jason, we should probably take her to a specialist and have her checked over thoroughly."

Jason nodded, and nothing more was said.

Meanwhile Cecily was worrying about her brother. She sent him a message:

Dear Randy,

# Rejoicing in Hope

> Daddy wrote me the bad news that you got yourself into trouble with the law. I am so sorry. I don't have any money, but if there is anything else I can do for you, just let me know. You're my favorite brother, you know.
>
> Love,
>
> Cecily

Randy Junior did not respond to her message, and Cecily, deeply involved in her studies and concerned about her aunt, let the matter go.

Gary returned from his partnership development meetings (support-raising) and began to urge her to set a date for their wedding. Originally they had planned to marry in October or November, but troubled as she was about her aunt's health and her brother's problem, Cecily hesitated to go ahead with their plans.

"Gary, I have another semester of studies after this, my brother is facing a legal crisis, and my Aunt Mary has health problems. She is the nearest thing I have to a mother, and I would like for her to have an important role in my wedding. Daddy will give me away, of course, but I'm not even sure that he wants to pay for my wedding.

Gary was silent. *I can see her point. Of course she's reluctant to make any definite plans for our wedding with these crises facing her, but I can't just sit here and kick my heels until Cecily's problems are all resolved. What should I do? Should I ask for a temporary field assignment or wait until Cecily is ready?*

*****

When Cecily informed Gary—during one of their telephone conversations—that she planned to visit her father

# Rejoicing in Hope

in Texarkana that weekend, he asked, "Are you planning to go alone?"

Surprised, Cecily was silent for a moment, then: "Will you be free that weekend?"

"I was planning to come home, yes."

"You haven't mentioned anything about that, so I didn't think I could plan on you going along." Cecily was ashamed to find that she would really prefer to go alone. Memories of the week Gary had spent with her in Texarkana rose in her mind's eye. Her father had objected to Cecily marrying a missionary and living in the jungle. *I think I would rather try to cope with Randy Junior's problem without Gary being there. Maybe Daddy would prefer that, too. What can I say?*

Gary interrupted her thoughts by saying, "Do you think your father would prefer that you come alone?"

Cecily was taken aback that Gary had read her thoughts so accurately. She was almost certain her father would prefer to see her alone, but she didn't want to say so. "One of the things Daddy wants to discuss with me is my brother's legal predicament. He got into debt and couldn't pay it. He got involved in some criminal activity trying to raise the money. I don't know how deeply he is involved. Would you like me to phone Daddy to ask whether you should come with me?"

Gary hesitated. "I don't imagine he wants an outsider in on this. Maybe if I drive up on Saturday we can play miniature golf or something like that? Would that be better?"

Cecily drew a deep breath of relief.

"I would appreciate that very much. I imagine Daddy must be eating his heart out over Randy Junior's stupid action."

*****

# Rejoicing in Hope

When Cecily arrived in Texarkana on the Friday evening, she found her father and step-mother at home.

"Is Randy Junior coming home tonight?" she asked.

Susan sniffed audibly, and her father answered quickly, "No, he's not here. If you want to see him, you should phone him at the dorm."

"You mean he's not coming home for the weekend? Where is he staying, then? The dining room closes over these weekends. I don't imagine he has very much money, if any."

Randy Senior looked sheepish. "I gave him a tongue lashing when I leaned about his misbehavior. He hasn't come home since."

"Did you invite him to come home?" Cecily wondered.

Susan broke in with, "I asked him whether he expected us to support him when he's behaving like this."

Randy Senior turned to look at his wife: "You asked what?"

"I asked him whether he thought we should keep on paying for his tuition, room and board when he does things like this."

"And did you say anything to him about not being welcome at home?"

Susan squirmed. "Not exactly, but when he has all his expenses paid, and then spends money like there's no tomorrow, it's bad enough. But then he tries to raise money illegally. That's even worse. I don't think we should pretend it didn't happen."

Randy Senior turned to Cecily: "Why don't you give him a call and invite him to come home. If he doesn't want to, maybe you could meet him at some hamburger joint for a meal."

## Rejoicing in Hope

Cecily nodded. She left the room to place her call.

She listened while Randy's phone rang eight times, and then she heard his voice, "Hello?"

"Hi, Randy. This is Cecily. I'm home, and I miss you. When are you coming?"

There was a short silence, and then:

"You're at the folks' house? Are you home for the weekend? When did you get there?"

"I just got here this afternoon and expected to see you when I got here. I miss you. When are you coming?"

"Well, Sis, I don't think the folks are expecting me to come home. I don't want to get thrown out on the street."

"We all miss you, Randy; I'm sure no one will throw you out, as you put it." Then she reflected that he might not have enough money to put gas into his car.

"Is there gas in your car? If not, I'll come by and pick you up."

"Maybe that would be best. I'll be waiting on the curb in front of the dorm."

When Cecily picked up her brother at the designated spot, she was surprised to see that he was coming empty-handed.

"Aren't you bringing anything for the overnight stay?"

Randy shrugged. "I'm not sure I'm staying overnight."

Cecily made no comment, but headed home.

# Rejoicing in Hope

## Chapter 30

Cecily and her brother rode several blocks in silence, then Randy Junior asked, "When did you get back from South America?"

"Last week. I've been back to classes in Dallas. When do your classes start?"

"They started this week, but I'm still not sure whether I can stay in school. I need to get a job, and they aren't easy to find."

Cecily turned to look at him. "What sort of job are you looking for?"

"I don't have a lot of choices. I suppose it'll have to be in some fast food joint. I've checked out a few, but they don't pay much, considering that I have to earn enough to pay my room and board as well as pay back the credit card debt."

"I wonder if Uncle Jason could help you find a job. Would you be willing to work in Dallas if he can find you a place there?"

"Do you think he would, if he knew the whole story?"

"I would think so, but since I don't know the 'whole story' myself, I can't be sure. There is one way to find out. Let's phone him tonight."

When Cecily pulled up at her father's driveway, Randy reluctantly stepped out of the car. His father must have been watching for him, because appeared at the front door, and smiled his welcome at his namesake.

"Welcome home, Son. Glad you could come."

# Rejoicing in Hope

Randy Junior mutely gripped his father's outstretched hand, and returned his father's embrace. Cecily fought back the tears that came to her eyes. *Just like the parable of the prodigal son!*[1]

Susan was waiting in the living room, and frowned at her stepson. "I hope you don't forget what you owe to your dad and me."

Randy Senior ignored this, and urged his children to join him in the den. "How are things going? Have you found a job yet?"

"Not yet. It's not easy, when I have this thing hanging over my head. Cecily was saying that our Uncle Jason might be able to help me find a job. I think she's going to check it out for me, right?" he turned to his sister.

Randy Senior interrupted.

"Do you plan to drop out of school? How can you work in Dallas and take classes in Texarkana?"

Randy Junior turned to answer his father's question. "I spent my grant money to pay back some of my credit card debt from the trip to Europe. I'm taking classes, but since I can't pay my tuition, I'll need to drop out. I have the dorm and cafeteria bills to pay, too."

"It won't hurt you to spend a semester working to pay your bills. I'm taking out a loan to pay your fine, but you'll have to pay me back. I don't have the kind of money I can throw away." Although Randy Senior's words were harsh, the tone of voice and expression on his face were not.

"I understand." Randy Junior's hazel eyes pleaded with his father. "I'm sorry I was so stupid…"

---

[1] Luke 15:11-32

## Rejoicing in Hope

Randy Senior scraped his throat to free the lump in it. "Sometimes we need to learn things the hard way."

Cecily excused herself and went to the living room to telephone the Nealeys. Her Uncle Jason answered the phone.

"Hello, Uncle Jason. How is Aunt Mary today?"

"Hi, Cecily. We're all right. Where are you calling from? Have you had car problems?"

Cecily laughed. "No, Uncle Jason. I'm at my dad's house, safe and sound. I picked up my brother at his dorm. He's been looking for a job and hasn't been too successful. I wondered if you know of any job for him."

"But he's attending college in Texarkana, isn't he? He can't very well attend classes there and work here in Dallas part time."

"Randy has apparently accumulated enough debts that he needs to drop out of school and work a semester to get them paid up. He and I were wondering whether you knew of a job for him where he could earn enough to pay room and board as well as making payments on his credit card debt."

"I see." Jason was silent for a moment, then: "What are his skills? What is his work experience?"

Cecily hesitated, probing her memory.

"I know he spent several summers working at a used car lot, making the cars more presentable to buyers. I don't think he worked during the semester, though. His major is in business administration."

"Let me see what I can do. Have Randy call me when he's available, OK?"

Cecily hung up the phone, and walked slowly back to the den. Randy was standing close to his father when she

## Rejoicing in Hope

entered. He looked up when she entered the room, and moved away from his father.

"You called Uncle Jason? What did he say?" Randy's voice was sharp with anxiety.

"He would like you to call him when you can. He says he'll see what he can do."

Randy's shoulders sagged a little.

"Well, that's that..."

Randy Senior interjected: "You can't expect more than that. He needs to see what openings he has, and whether your qualifications match them. I think his response is encouraging."

"Maybe so...." Randy shrugged.

Cecily wanted to ask her brother how he had managed to become so hopelessly in debt, but she knew he would resent the question. *Credit card debt snowballs.*

Randy Senior scraped his throat and suggested, "See if your stepmother has our supper ready. After that, we'll ask Cecily to show-and-tell us about her trip to Brazil."

Randy Jr. ran to the kitchen to check with Susan. Cecily went out to her car and pulled the mementos of her visit to South America out of her trunk, which included snapshots, clay pots (very fragile), mesh bags and fishing nets made by the Guará Indians. When they finished their supper, Cecily sat back and began to tell about her experiences.

*****

When she finished, Susan said, "Indians everywhere are dirty and lazy. They seem to care for nothing but painting their bodies, dancing, and getting drunk."

# Rejoicing in Hope

Randy Senior disagreed. "This kind of demoralization is often the result of domination by an aggressive society and the subsequent loss of the minority people's lands and traditions. Cecily just reminded us that the Portuguese colonizers introduced alcohol to the Guará tribe in order to dominate them."

*****

When Gary drove up to Texarkana on Saturday, he invited Randy to join Cecily and himself in a miniature golf game. After the game they stopped at a drive-in and enjoyed banana splits. Then Gary returned to Cedar Hill, while Cecily drove Randy back to his dorm, before returning to the Nealey home in Cedar Hill. She had the satisfaction of knowing that her father and brother had been reconciled, but she still did not know how her brother was to solve his financial problems.

When she arrived back in Cedar Hill, her Uncle Jason told her he had already notified Randy that he had a place for him in the shipping warehouse, and that he was welcome to stay with the Nealey family until he was well established in his job. As a consequence, a grateful Randy moved down to Cedar Hill and into the Nealey home. Cecily warned him that he would have to take care of himself, because their aunt was unwell and she herself would not have time to wait on him because of the pressure of her class assignments. She was relieved to find that he took her at her word, and not only kept his room clean but washed and dried his own clothes. He also took time to entertain his little cousin Jay in the evenings.

*****

Mary's Mega-literacy course was in its final two weeks, and she struggled to keep ahead of her students.

# Rejoicing in Hope

Cecily found her aunt looking paler than ever, but Mary refused to drop out of her part of the course. She had bowed to her family's wishes, however, and made an appointment with a gastroenterologist for the week after the literacy course ended. She admitted to Cecily that she didn't see much sense in running to doctors for help in dealing with her digestive problems, but said that she was willing to see the doctor because Jason was worrying about her.

"I think it's just something I have to go through by myself. If I can find out which foods are giving me problems, and avoid them, I should be all right," she told her niece.

On the day of the appointment Cecily came home to find a troubled aunt in the kitchen preparing supper. When Cecily asked her what the doctor had said, she shrugged her shoulders.

"The doctor scheduled me for ultrasounds tests, an MRI, a CAT scan, and a colonoscopy. I am having some blood tests, as well. Jason and I had planned to take a vacation next week in Galveston, but now I have to stay around here until I've taken all these tests," she complained. "I'd like to take a vacation first, but Jason says no. He says I need to take the tests as soon as possible. But if the results all come back normal, I'll know I'm just a hypochondriac."

Cecily laughed in spite of herself.

"I think it would be a relief if that were the case. Let me know what I can do to help."

Mary took all the diagnostic tests over a period of three weeks. Then Jason took her to a resort in Galveston on the Gulf of Mexico. There they rested while they awaited the results of her diagnostic tests. She left little Jay in Cecily's and Randy's care. Randy took him to school in the mornings, and Cecily picked him up at 2 PM and brought him home.

# Rejoicing in Hope

She fixed him a snack, and then he ran outdoors to play with the neighbor boys. This allowed Cecily time to work on her class assignments without interruptions. When Randy came home from work, he took over his little cousin's care, gave him a bath, and got him ready for bed. Jay glowed with pleasure under his cousins' care.

Mary phoned regularly to find out how little Jay was getting along. She reported that she found the cooler weather of the Gulf refreshing and enjoyed the beautiful grounds of the spa. They were scheduled to return to Cedar Hill on Monday.

On Friday Cecily received a message by voice mail from the gastroenterologist's office. The physician's assistant left word that the doctor would like to see Mrs. Nealey in his office to share the results of the tests she had undergone. Cecily knew of no previous engagements her aunt had, so she tentatively set up an appointment for Tuesday morning, the day after Mary was scheduled to return.

# Rejoicing in Hope

# Rejoicing in Hope

## Chapter 31

That following Monday Cecily picked up little Jay at his elementary school at 2 PM and drove home. She noticed that the Nealey's garage door was open, and Jason's car was back in its place. *They're back home! I wonder how Aunt Mary is doing.*

Little Jay also noticed that his father's car was in the garage, and jumped up and down in his car seat in his excitement.

"Mommy and Daddy are home!" and he struggled to release the restraining belt on his car seat.

"Wait," Cecily cautioned, "wait until I park the car. Don't try to get out until I do."

"Hurry," urged Jay, "I want to get out."

Cecily parked the car and helped little Jay out of the car. He dashed into the house and called, "Mommy, Daddy!"

"I'm here in the kitchen," his mother called. She came out and gathered her little son in her arms. Cecily came in and greeted her aunt with a hug. She noticed that Mary seemed rested; her coloring was better, and she had even gotten a little suntan. Little Jay was clamoring for his mother's attention, so Cecily stepped back and greeted Jason.

"She looks a lot better. How has she been feeling?"

Jason shrugged. "She has her ups and downs. She doesn't eat much and hasn't put on any weight, but she has been sleeping better."

## Rejoicing in Hope

"Did you remember that you have an appointment with the specialist tomorrow morning? He wants to discuss the results of the various tests with you both."

Jason nodded. "I know. Thanks for setting that up for us."

Little Jay was trying to describe all the fun things he had done during his parents' absence, and then he told his mother about the times he fell, and the minor mishaps he had suffered, and added in the same breath, "And Randy is going to take me to the miniature golf course tonight, when he gets home from work."

Jason interrupted with "Haven't you got even one hug for your dad?" and picked his son up in his arms.

Little Jay laughed and wrapped his arms around his father's neck.

*****

On Tuesday afternoon little Jay took a long time to calm down enough to eat his after-school snack. He went outside to wait for his parents to come home. When his parents came he was playing with a neighbor boy, and, after shouting "Hi Mommy, hi Daddy!" he returned to his play.

Cecily was struggling with her language assignment when she heard the car drive up. She hurried down the stairs, and when she saw the faces of her uncle and aunt, she realized that the results of the tests had been an unpleasant shock to them. Her uncle silently helped his wife up the stairs. Cecily was burning to ask them what they had learned from the doctor, but bit back the words. She returned to her room and knelt by her bed.

*Lord, I don't know what the tests showed, but I know that they both look as though the news was pretty bad. Give them strength and give me wisdom.*

# Rejoicing in Hope

Mary did not leave her room during the remainder of the day, and Jason spent several hours at her bedside. When little Jay came in from play he crawled up on his parents' bed.

Randy came home from work at the usual time. He knocked on their door, and reminded little Jay that they had planned to play miniature golf that evening. Jay asked his mother's permission, and she gave it gladly.

After Randy and Jay left, Jason went downstairs to his study to make some phone calls dealing with urgent business. Cecily tried to get back to her studies, but found it hard to concentrate. *What can the doctor have told them that makes them look so sad?*

A short while later Cecily heard Mary call her name. When Cecily entered her aunt's bedroom she noticed that Mary looked as though she had been crying. Cecily felt shy and pretended she had not noticed. She asked, "Would you like something to eat, Aunt Mary?"

Mary said, "Just a bowl of soup, I think." Then, as Cecily turned to leave, she said, "Wait, Cecily. I need to tell you what the doctor said. I don't want to spread it around yet, nor do I want to talk about it in front of Little Jay, but I think you need to know."

Cecily nodded. Mary continued, "The doctor says he's not completely sure what it is, but that the tests show that I have some kind of liver disease. It may be benign, like cirrhosis, or malignant, like a cancer. He's referring me to an oncologist—a cancer specialist—to make a definite diagnosis. He says there are treatments that help temporarily, but there is no known cure. In uncomplicated cirrhosis a liver transplant may resolve the problem. In the case of cancer, if there's only one tumor in the very early stages, it can be removed by surgery, although not all doctors agree that this is worthwhile."

# Rejoicing in Hope

Mary drew a shuddering breath and went on, "I think if it were not for little Jay, I might be more resigned to this prospect. It's easy to talk about being ready to die, but it isn't easy to face it and to realize that I am leaving a young son behind who will certainly miss his mother. Pray for me, Cecily!"

Cecily stood rooted to the floor. She stared at her aunt uncomprehendingly. *It's impossible! Did my aunt Mary just tell me that she had an incurable liver disease? Surely I didn't hear aright.* Thoughts raced crazily through her mind. She was recalled by her aunt: "Cecily, I don't want to forget to thank you for taking such good care of Jay while we were away. Apparently Randy has really won his heart. I thank you both very much."

Cecily, dazed, was unsure what she should do. She wanted to hug her aunt, but her feet would not move. Suddenly aware that her aunt was expecting some kind of response from her, she stammered, "Y-you're welcome. We enjoyed it."

She went downstairs to the kitchen to fix the soup for Mary, but her thoughts still tumbled chaotically through her head. She turned and headed for the den, where Jason was now jotting notes on a pad. He looked up when she walked in.

"Uncle Jason, Aunt Mary just told me the doctor thinks she may have cancer. What do you think?"

Jason sighed. "It doesn't sound good, but the doctor isn't really sure what it is, so I don't know why we should assume the worst. He admits he could be wrong. We certainly need to see an oncologist as soon as we can get an appointment so that we can know for sure, one way or another."

# Rejoicing in Hope

Cecily turned and went to the kitchen, cheered by her uncle's optimism. *It can't be true that she has cancer. It can't be. It's all a mistake.*

*****

The oncologist to whom the gastroenterologist referred Mary, had no openings for two weeks. At first this delay in knowing her definite diagnosis seemed almost intolerable, but Mary got busy with projects that she had put aside during the Mega-Literacy course. Several days after her return, she said to Cecily, "Gary and you talked about getting married soon. Are you still planning on that?"

Cecily looked surprised. "Well, Gary is urging me to start planning for it, but I don't want to do it while you aren't feeling well."

"That's considerate of you, but I think we do well to start our planning. I know Gary wants to go to the field sometime next year, and you'll need some time to get adjusted to each other before you go. The translation mission doesn't like to send newlyweds right out to the field."

"Are you sure you're up to the excitement, Aunt Mary?"

Mary smiled. "It will be nice to have happy excitement instead of stress from health problems. I think we could begin by looking for a wedding dress."

Cecily felt the stirring of excitement welling up.

"That would be fun, but I don't know whether Daddy wants to pay for the wedding, or if he does, how large a wedding he's willing to pay for. Maybe I should call him and find out."

"We certainly don't want to exclude your father from this once-in-a-lifetime event. I'm sure he'll want to be involved in the choices. We can have the wedding just the way Gary and you want it."

## Rejoicing in Hope

"I guess we could start with the wedding gown. Maybe we could even decide on a date and place for the wedding. I'll send Gary an e-mail to get his input."

When she sent Gary an e-mail message to ask for his input as to wedding dates, she received a return call from him after only one day.

"What's this, Cecily? Have some of your problems been resolved? How's Randy doing? Is your Aunt Mary feeling better?"

"Randy Junior is here in Cedar Hill. He's working for my Uncle Jason in the warehouse. He seems to be happy enough. And Aunt Mary just returned from a vacation in Galveston, where she absolutely relished the cooler weather. She has an appointment with an oncologist two weeks from now. I was hesitant about planning our wedding, but she insists that she would enjoy helping to plan it, so we plan to shop for a wedding gown this coming Saturday. I haven't talked to Daddy yet about how much we can spend on the wedding, but I would think that a simple wedding would be better. I don't want a big splash. What about you?"

Gary fervently seconded her opinion, and Cecily phoned her father to discuss the wedding plans with him. He merely asked, "Are you sure this is what you want to do, Cessy?" He used the pet name that Randy Junior used to call her.

Cecily swallowed her emotion.

"Yes, Daddy. I'm sure. I love Gary, and I want to be involved in the same ministry he is in. This is what I want."

"In that case, you can charge me for the wedding. If you can keep the cost under five thousand dollars, I would appreciate it very much."

Cecily smiled. "I think I can, Daddy. I'll try, anyway."

*****

# Rejoicing in Hope

Cecily and Gary set a date and decided to have the wedding in Cedar Hill in the church in which both had been baptized. The women's society of the church—one of the church's ministries—volunteered to host the marriage reception in the Fellowship Hall. The engaged couple scheduled their obligatory premarital counseling sessions with the pastor, and chose their attendants. Paula was to be Cecily's Maid of Honor, and Cecily's college roommate and a classmate from the Graduate Linguistics Center were her bridesmaids. Randy Junior was to be one of the ushers, and Gary's cousin Bill was the second usher. Gary chose his best friend Walter to be his Best Man.

Cecily was amazed to see how everything seemed to fall into place. The only planning that was left to do was who must be put on the wedding guest list.

A furloughing missionary couple was heading back overseas, and offered their Dallas apartment to them for six months. The engaged couple planned a week's honeymoon in Galveston, and then would return to set up housekeeping in Dallas, where Cecily would take her comprehensive exams for the master's degree of arts in linguistics.

Sometime after graduation Cecily would need to take the jungle survival course in Mexico, where Gary—having already taken the course— would serve on the staff. Then Cecily would accompany Gary on partnership development trips until the pledges of support reached the quota requirements of the Brazil Branch. After the goal had been reached the couple would head to Brazil to take up their assignment.

# Rejoicing in Hope

# Rejoicing in Hope

## Chapter 32

Mary's two-week-long wait to see the oncologist finally ended, and Jason took Mary to her appointment with Dr. Spencer.

The Nealeys took their seats in the waiting room. Mary had kept herself so busy helping Cecily with her wedding plans that she had been able to push the worries about her health to the background and ignore the threat that hung over her head. Now, as she sat in the silent waiting room with perhaps half a dozen other equally silent people, she could no longer evade the fact that the black shadow of a pending diagnosis hung over her. She turned to Jason: "Jason..."

Jason turned to her, and saw the shadow of fear in her eyes. He reached over and took her hand in his.

"I'm here, Sweetheart. I'll always be here for you."

Mary swallowed the lump in her throat. Unable to speak, she merely nodded and squeezed his hand.

It seemed like forever, but it was probably only fifteen minutes before they were called into the doctor's examining room. There a physician's assistant took Mary's vital signs, and told them to wait, because the "doctor will be with you shortly."

Mary studied the posters on the walls of the examining room that depicted normal body organs contrasted with diseased organs. *God, I trust my life and my future to you, whether it will be short or long...."*

After another wait of fifteen minutes, the oncologist knocked gently on the closed door and entered the room, introducing himself to the tense couple anxiously waiting for him. Dr. Spencer was a tall, slender man with a receding

## Rejoicing in Hope

hairline. He smiled at them both, and asked Mary to lie down on the examination table. He palpated her abdomen, paying special attention to the upper right side. Then he said, "I've studied the results of the tests you underwent, and we'll talk about them in a minute. But first, I want to know if you have ever had a drinking problem? Have you ever been diagnosed with cancer anywhere in your body? In your breast? Your stomach? Your colon?"

"No, sir," Mary responded. "I never drank, and I've never been diagnosed with cancer. Never."

"The reason why I asked is because you definitely have cancer of the liver, but it is a kind of cancer that normally is secondary to a primary cancer somewhere else in the body, such as breast cancer, for example. The CAT scan and MRI tests show what may be a primary malignancy in your colon."

Mary felt that the breath had been sucked out of her body. She could only shake her head.

Jason interrupted, "Are you sure, doctor?"

Dr. Spencer nodded. "The cancer is far enough advanced that there can be no doubt about it. For your sakes, I wish there were."

"What kind of treatments are available? How about surgery or chemotherapy or radiation treatments?" Mary struggled to pull herself out of the fog that seemed to be settling over her mind.

"There are several treatments, but they don't seem to be effective in modifying the outcome of the disease. They're costly and are almost as painful as the disease itself. They're available, but I don't recommend them."

"How long, doctor?" Jason's voice seemed to come from a long way off.

# Rejoicing in Hope

"Probably six months at the most. We can prescribe some medications to try to make you more comfortable, but that is about all we can hope for."

The doctor went on to prescribe follow-up appointments and wrote out prescriptions for palliative medications, but Mary heard nothing. She sat as if frozen, unable to think. Jason received the prescriptions and sheet of instructions from the doctor, some free samples from the physician's assistant, and led Mary out of the office to their parked car.

As he closed the driver's door behind him, Jason bent over the steering wheel and groaned, "Oh Lord, is this what lies ahead for us?"

Mary was mute. She looked like a wounded animal.

After a few moments, she turned to Jason, "Let's not go home right away. Let's drive over to the Mountain Creek Lake and pray."

*****

Cecily picked up little Jay from his school and brought him home. He looked around for his mother, and seemed very disappointed. "Where's Mommy, Cessy?"

"She went to see the doctor, but they should be home by the time you take a little snack."

"Where's Daddy?"

"He went with Mommy to see the doctor, and they'll be coming home together." Cecily noticed that Jay was looking worried.

"Why did they go to see the doctor?" he asked.

"Because Mommy has been having a lot of tummy aches. You remember that, don't you?" Jay nodded and said no more.

# Rejoicing in Hope

After his snack Jay waited outdoors for his parents to return. Cecily tried to return to her studies, but as the minutes passed and they did not return, she began to fear the worst. Jay came in the back door and called for his mother.

"She hasn't come home yet, Jay. We'll have to wait a little while yet."

"But you said she'd be here after I'd had my snack, and that was a long time ago!" His tone said "you promised."

"True, I did say that, but I was wrong. I guess we'll have to wait a little longer."

Jay said no more, and went out in the yard again to watch for his parents' return.

It was five o'clock before the family car drove up and parked in the garage. Jay ran to greet his mother as she got out of the car.

"Mommy! You're home!" and he threw his arms around her.

Mary's pale face lighted up at the welcome she received from her son. "Yes, I'm home, and very glad to be home. Have you had your snack today?"

"Yes, I ate lots, but you weren't here and I wanted you," Jay insisted.

"And I wanted you. Where is Cecily?"

Cecily had heard the car drive up and hurried downstairs to greet her uncle and aunt. "I'm here, and glad to see you. Did you have a long wait to see the doctor?"

"No, not too long, but we decided to drive over to the Mountain Creek Lake because we wanted a quiet place to pray."

## Rejoicing in Hope

Cecily nodded. "Come on in. I suppose you're hungry? I've got the food ready to fix for supper. Would you like some coffee and carrot cake while I fix supper?"

Mary hesitated. "I think I'd prefer some hot tea to take with the carrot cake." As Jason joined them, she asked him, "Would you like to have some tea with me, or would you prefer coffee?"

Jason put his arm around his wife. "I'll have some tea with you," he said.

Cecily paused a moment to look at her aunt, whose face showed some traces of tears, and then she turned around to enter the kitchen and put the teakettle on the stove for tea. *Apparently the news was bad, and they needed some time alone to come to terms with it.*

She put the teacups on the kitchen table and cut the carrot cake. Little Jay crept in his mother's lap, and she seemed to draw comfort from his little arms clinging to her. Cecily withdrew and went to her own room. *Oh God, I don't understand. They're such a happy family and show so much love to the world. Why would you tear them apart and cause so much grief and pain?*

\*\*\*\*\*

That evening, as Cecily downloaded her e-mail, she found a message from Rachel Kruyter:

Dear Cecily,

> Not a day passes, but the children ask me where you are, and when you will be coming back. We really miss you. I understand that Gary and you will request to be assigned to Brazil, so maybe we will see you again in another year or so.

# Rejoicing in Hope

Your language teacher Adela is still ailing; she never returned to her previous health. Apparently she suffered some internal injuries during the binge. She is still quite thin and wasted-looking. She often asks me when you are coming back.

How is your Aunt Mary? We haven't heard from her lately, but she wrote me a few months ago that she was having some digestive problems. By now her course must be over, so I hope she is feeling better, too.

Write and tell me the latest news from Texas. We haven't had much excitement here since Jerry poked a horse in the genitals with a stick, and got a swift kick in the head in retaliation. Thank the Lord, it was only an external bruise. It could have been much worse.

Have you set the date for your wedding yet? If I remember correctly, you talked about getting married some time early next year. We're praying for you.

Love,

Rachel, for Richard, Laura Marie, Jerry, and Hannah

Cecily sat down at her computer to answer Rachel's message.

Dear Rachel, Richard, Laura Marie, Jerry, and Hannah,

I was glad to hear from you. Let me tell you some news from here.

# Rejoicing in Hope

Aunt Mary is not well. She consulted with several doctors, the last one being an oncologist. He diagnosed her liver and colon problem, and says there isn't much that can be done for her, except to try to make her more comfortable. She doesn't want the diagnosis to be talked about, mostly because she doesn't want little Jay to hear it from other people. I know she would appreciate your prayers.

Gary and I have set the wedding date for January fourth, early in the New Year. We've reserved the auditorium of our church for the event. Aunt Mary and I went shopping and bought my wedding gown. We found a beautiful one at a used clothing store that needs only a few tucks to fit perfectly. The women of the church will cater our wedding reception. I was reluctant to plan the wedding because Aunt Mary is unwell, but she wanted to have a part in planning it, so things are pretty much settled, except for the guest list.

My brother Randy has gotten himself into trouble and has a credit card debt. He had to drop out of school and now is living with the Nealeys. He's working in Uncle Jason's warehouse, trying to earn enough to pay his debt. He seems to have settled in well.

Uncle Jason and Aunt Mary send their love, and we pray for you every day.

Love,

Cecily

# Rejoicing in Hope

# Rejoicing in Hope

## Chapter 33

The following day Randy bathed little Jay and turned him over to his mother for his bedtime story and prayers. Then he tapped on Cecily's door.

Cecily opened the door. "Hi, Randy! What's new?"

Randy stepped inside the room and closed the door behind him.

"Cessy, what did Aunt Mary find out when she went to the doctor? Everything is so hush-hush, and no one says anything, but I'd like to know what the doctor told them."

Cecily sighed.

"The reason no one talks about her diagnosis is that she doesn't want word to get around to little Jay. We're 'hushed,' as you say, so that Jay won't overhear something that could scare him. I'm sure she wouldn't mind if I told you, but she doesn't want us to talk about it."

Randy listened to this explanation in silence, then he said, "Does she have cancer, or something like that?"

Cecily nodded. "Cancer of the colon and liver, and the doctor has given her six months to live, at the most."

Randy paled. "Are you serious? What an awful thing to hear. And the doctor *told* her that?"

"Yes, but that isn't all. There isn't anything they can do for her. She's just shattered, knowing that she'll have to leave little Jay behind."

Randy shook his head. "It must be awful to know you're going to die in half a year. How can anybody face that?"

# Rejoicing in Hope

"She believes that she is going to be with the Lord. When she was a teenager she knelt and asked the Lord to receive her. She believes that he did, and that he'll walk her through this death process. Her heart aches for little Jay, though. How he will miss her!"

Randy looked at his sister. "Does being a Christian mean that you're not afraid to die?"

Cecily nodded. "Being a real Christian means that you've asked God to forgive your sins and receive you because Christ died for you. I did that when I was a junior in college. Have you ever asked God to forgive you, Randy?"

He shook his head. "No, I'm not religious. I never go to church—at least, I didn't until I came to live here. Then Uncle Jason said he expected me to go to church with the family, so I do. I don't mind going to church, but God is just a mystery to me."

Cecily looked at him with concern. "God loves you, and he sent his Son to die on the cross so that you could be accepted as his child and spend eternity with him. Those who refuse to confess their sins and ask God's forgiveness will go to the place of eternal punishment because they've rejected his offer. If you want to know God, you need to do it on his terms."[1]

"And what are those terms?" Randy sounded skeptical.

"Uncle Jason could explain those terms a lot better than I can, but I know that God is far above us, and that he can't accept sin. But because he loved us, he sent Jesus Christ, his only Son, into the world. He died on the cross to pay the price of our sins, so that God could accept us. If you want to know God, you need to kneel and pray, asking him to show you how you can know him. And read your Bible. I know

---

[1] John 3:16-18

# Rejoicing in Hope

Aunt Mary gave you one years ago. The Bible tells us what we need to know about God, but only God can make himself real to you."[1]

Randy backed off and opened the door. He mumbled, "Thanks, Cessy. I'll think about it."

As the door closed behind Randy, Cecily stood motionless where he had left her. She bowed her head and prayed silently for her brother.

*****

The following day Cecily was working at her computer, preparing her class assignments, when her aunt rapped on the open door of her room. Cecily jumped up.

"Aunt Mary! Is there something I can do for you?"

Mary smiled. Her face was wan and pale, but she looked tranquil. "I just wanted to talk to you, if you can spare me the time."

"Of course." Cecily thought, *she wants us to postpone our wedding because she doesn't feel well enough to handle all the fuss and busyness of it.* She offered her chair to her aunt, and sat on the edge of her bed facing her.

"I just wondered how you are doing on the wedding plans. As I remember, you lack only the guest list, and we do have to get at it, because it's likely to be complicated. It's not always easy to agree about who should be asked and who should not."

Cecily stared. "Maybe we should put it off for a while. I think it may be too much for you."

Mary smiled again. "I say, let's get to working on the list as soon as possible. We need to get input from the

---

[1] John 6:44-47

# Rejoicing in Hope

Ballards as well as from your father. We probably should keep the list down to something like a hundred, because of the size of the fellowship room where we hope to hold the reception."

"But Aunt Mary, it doesn't seem right to have a big celebration when you're feeling so poorly." Cecily struggled to put her thoughts into words without saying "we should wait until after your die." *That's not much of an option, either.*

"I know, but you're like a daughter to me, and I'd like to see you happily married and doing what the Lord called you to do before I go."

Cecily yielded. "You're the nearest thing I have to a mother, and I'd love to have you take part in my wedding as much as you feel you can. How about this weekend? I have some papers to finish that are due on Friday, but on Saturday maybe we can sit down with Mrs. Ballard and work on a list. I'll phone Daddy and get his input."

Mary agreed. "I'll set it up with Jean and get back to you."

The following day Cecily downloaded a message from Rachel Kruyter:

> Dear Cecily,
>
> Your message left me gasping for air. Somehow I never expected anything like that to happen to my friend Mary. My first impulse was to get an airline reservation and come to see you, but I realize that with three young children (not to mention a husband) it would not be easy for me to do that. From what you say, I gather that, while she is miserable with her digestive discomfort, she is still active in many things. I remember

## Rejoicing in Hope

when my mother was diagnosed with breast cancer that I felt my world had come to an end, but after surgery, chemotherapy, and radiation, she returned to normal. Is there such a prospect for your aunt? I seem to remember that cancer of the liver is harder to treat than breast cancer. Also it seems to appear more as a metastasis from other organs, like from breast cancer. I will need to get more information, probably from the Internet.

I am so glad that she has you. Wasn't God good to bring you to live with the Nealeys, to help them through this very rough patch! I think your decision to go on with the wedding plans is a good one, since it means so much to Mary.

We will certainly pray for all of you. Do, please, keep me informed. And if you need me, I know God will open up a way for me to be there, however impossible that seems now. In spite of all our troubles, God is good.

Love,

Rachel

Cecily swallowed the lump in her throat, and bowed her head. *Lord, help me. I don't know how to be a help and comfort to the family. Give me wisdom, please!*

*****

Randy was working with another employee in the storage room, when his colleague lost his grip on a large carton, and dropped it on his foot. Jason was entering the room just as the employee let out a string of profane epithets. Prominently featured in the words was God's name. Jason

# Rejoicing in Hope

stopped, helped the employee to pick up the carton and move it to the target spot. He checked the sufferer's foot for bruises. There were apparently no fractures or dislocations. Then he turned to him and said gently, "I understand why you're upset, but I heard you use God's name in a way that I can't allow on my premises."

George sputtered. "It doesn't mean anything. I just swore because I hurt my foot badly."

Jason nodded. "I understand that. But if I used your name whenever I was upset, in the way you used God's name just now, would you be pleased?"

"No," George admitted, "but it doesn't mean anything."

"Would it mean something to you, if you were listening when I used your name in that way?"

"I wouldn't like it," George admitted.

"It's much worse when we use God's name carelessly or profanely. He is high above us, and he insists that we need to respect his name. That's what the third commandment of the law is about: not to misuse his name. It's number three of God's Big Ten rules, right up there with murder and stealing."

Jason turned and left the storage area. Randy stared after him. *I wonder why he came here in the first place.* "I guess he forgot what he came for."

George muttered something incoherent in response, but returned limping to his work.

At the supper table Randy was very quiet. Jason, never much of a talker, noticed that his nephew was unusually silent. Normally Randy carried his share of the table conversation, but today he seemed lost in thought. After supper Randy bathed his little cousin as was his custom, and

## Rejoicing in Hope

after turning him over to his mother, he sought his uncle in the den.

Jason looked up at Randy's entrance, and smiled to encourage him.

"What's up, Randy?"

"I've been thinking."

Jason nodded to encourage him, and waited.

"It's about God." He found the religious topic embarrassing, and blurted out, "Why is his name so special?"

"Because God is so special. There is no one like him. Not only is he so great, but he is so good. We love him and we worship him because he is God. Because of whom he is, and because of what he has done for us, we need to use God's name reverently." He picked up his Bible, flipped to a page, and read:

> Therefore, since we are receiving a kingdom that cannot be shaken, let us be thankful, and so worship God acceptably with reverence and awe, for our "God is a consuming fire."[1]

Randy hesitated, and then plunged into his dilemma.

"Cecily says that if we want to know God we have to do it on his terms. She says that God can't accept us the way we are, but we need to ask him to forgive us. What I don't get is what God's terms are for getting to know him."

Jason drew a deep breath and lifted a silent prayer to God. He held the Bible in his hands.

"We can know what God is like by studying what the Bible says about him. But to know him personally, we must

---

[1] Hebrews 12:28, 29

## Rejoicing in Hope

ask God to reveal himself to us. We need to ask him on our knees." He opened his Bible and read:

> And without faith it is impossible to please God, because anyone who comes to him must believe that he exists and that he rewards those who earnestly seek him.[1]

"But how can anyone find God? How can we find someone so great, so invisible, so, so remote?"

Jason nodded. "It would be impossible to find him on our own, if it were not for the fact that he is seeking us. Do you remember the parable of the lost sheep?"

Randy shook his head. He had probably heard it sometime in his life, but couldn't honestly remember any details.

Jason opened his Bible and read the parable of the lost sheep to him.[2] Then he explained: "The shepherd went after the lost sheep. The reason why we sense a deep desire to seek for God is because he is already seeking for us. He has put the desire to know him in your heart. You need to respond and reach out to him in humility. Ask him to forgive your sins and receive you. Would you like to kneel with me and ask him now?"

Randy nodded mutely. Jason invited him to kneel with him, and together they asked God to reveal himself to Randy.

---

[1] Hebrews 11:6
[2] Luke 15:3-7

# Rejoicing in Hope

## Chapter 34

The project of making a list of people to invite to the wedding was about as complicated as is normally the case. Jean Ballard's list had to be trimmed, as was the case with Mary's. Cecily's father had offered only a few names, but his wife Susan made a list of her own, many of the people on the list Cecily did not know and could see no reason to invite. After skimming the list she phoned Susan and tried to explain tactfully why her list had been drastically reduced.

"It was good of you to put so much work into finding names of people you believe should be invited to our wedding. I know you put a lot of thought into it. However, we're trying to keep the list down to right around one hundred names, because the fellowship room—where we're having the wedding reception—only holds about one hundred fifty people. That number would include the servers, as well as the wedding party. Everyone else is having their list trimmed, too. I imagine that it will have to be a much smaller event than most people expect. Even if we had the reception in a larger hall, I would want to keep the list down, because my Aunt Mary, who is helping me with the planning, is not well and out of consideration for her we're keeping the reception small."

Cecily could imagine her stepmother's reaction, but was spared her comments because she hung up, and did not reply to her stepdaughter's apology.

Mary offered to order the wedding invitations, so Cecily was able to concentrate on her studies again. She also needed to study for her comprehensive exams which were scheduled for late January, after the couple returned from their brief honeymoon.

## Rejoicing in Hope

Gary had finished his tour of duty representing the translation mission to churches and seminaries. He was now assigned to work in the Dallas regional office and was living at home. This meant that Cecily could see him whenever she wished, but with the pressure of studies and the domestic duties she had taken over from her ailing aunt, she found herself carrying a heavy load. Seeing this, Gary took over the responsibility of helping Mary Nealey with the wedding preparations. He was relieved to find that Cecily was not asking to postpone the wedding until a later date.

In November Cecily and Randy Junior were surprised by a visit from their father. He explained it thus: "I never get to see either of my kids nowadays, so I came to see how you're doing."

Since Randy had more free time than Cecily, who was studying for her final exams, he took it upon himself to take his father around town and he showed him where the wedding celebration would take place. The Ballards invited them to supper, and Randy Senior found some of his worries dissipating after interacting with his future son-in-law's family. On the final evening of his visit to Cedar Hill he took his daughter out for a leisurely dinner, and expressed his satisfaction with the improvement he had seen in his son, and his appreciation for his future son-in-law.

"Watching you help your aunt and seeing Randy doing so well, I realize how much I owe to your Aunt Mary and her husband. I also am proud of the man you chose. He seems to be the kind of man most women would like to have for a husband. The one who has changed the most is your brother. He's gained a lot of maturity in the short time he's been here."

"I think you deserve a lot of credit for that, Dad. I know that he appreciates the way you handled his short path into deviation. Uncle Jason deserves credit there, too. Randy

## Rejoicing in Hope

really looks up to him. Above all, I believe that God deserves credit for shaping up our lives."

"Maybe so." Randy Senior was silent for a moment. "When I was little your grandmother stopped taking us to church, and I think I stopped believing in God. I wondered if he even existed."

"And now...?"

Randy Shears shrugged. "Now I think he probably does, after all."

Cecily looked at him and wondered what difference, if any, it would make in her father's life. She didn't know how to express this thought without offending him, so she said nothing.

*****

Two weeks before Christmas Mary suffered a relapse. She began vomiting and was unable to keep any food down. She was briefly hospitalized. The burden of the family's care fell entirely on Cecily's shoulders. Randy stepped in and did the grocery shopping while Jason divided his time between his wife and his business. The three of them (Jason, Cecily, and Randy) cooperated to care for little Jay. When Jason brought Mary home after three days she was visibly thinner and there was a yellowish cast to her skin. Thereafter visiting nurses came to the Nealey home every day to supervise her care and Jason set up a hospital bed in the spare bedroom downstairs for her.

Jean Ballard invited the Nealey family and the Spears siblings over to her home for Christmas dinner. Her daughters helped prepare the food, and a folding recliner was set up in a corner of the dining room for Mary. Cecily offered to contribute the Nealey's share to the feast, but Jean refused her offer.

## Rejoicing in Hope

"You have enough on your hands with your studies and keeping the household running. You also have to get ready for your wedding right after the New Year. Maybe you can help fix the Christmas dinner next year...if you're still around."

That week Randy approached his uncle and offered: "I'd be happy to move out of your house, if that would make things easier for you folks."

Jason lifted harassed eyes to his nephew.

"I'll check with Cecily, but my perception is that you're an asset to the family. You help with the housework and with little Jay. We would miss you if you left. If you don't mind staying on until after the wedding, at least, I'd appreciate it."

Randy nodded. "I'll be glad to stay as long as I can be a help."

*****

As the time for the wedding approached, the women's society of the church started bringing a main meal to the Nealey house every day. Cecily was deeply grateful, because she was trying to finish off her semester assignments and readying the apartment for their occupancy as newlyweds. Randy had virtually taken over the care of little Jay, but Mary faithfully kept to the story hour and prayer time with him every evening.

Gary was spending more time helping Cecily, doing the necessary shopping, and turning his hand to housekeeping. When Cecily asked him if he was used to doing housework, he grinned, "No, but I'm sure I'll have to get used to it after we're married. You have your studies to complete and your Comp exams to do after we get home from our honeymoon."

# Rejoicing in Hope

Cecily smiled at him and gave him a quick kiss. "I'll probably have to spend some time with Aunt Mary, too. She's almost halfway on her journey Home."

Gary looked at his fiancée with tenderness.

"I remember how you walked with your grandmother on her last mile. You're the most wonderful girl I ever met. How did I get so blessed that I can have you as my wife?"

Cecily crept into his arms, and they were silent for a time. Then she said, "I think I'm the lucky one. Even Daddy thinks that other women will envy me."

"Did he really say that? I thought he didn't like me because I was taking his little girl to an unhealthy jungle to live." Gary was remembering his first visit to the Spears family.

Cecily laughed. "Actually, he likes you better now that he has met your family. They really impressed him."

"That figures. They *are* wonderful, but they've had problems, too. Did I ever tell you that my parents were separated for about a year when Mary first came to live with us?"

"Really?" Cecily lifted her head from his shoulder and looked at him in surprise. "Why was that?"

"I never really knew why. He moved in with a young chick for a while, but when she left him he decided to come home again."

Cecily studied his face. "I remember when Daddy moved out. You probably know that my mother started sleeping around and doing drugs when Randy and I were little. We lived with our mother, but sometimes she would be gone all night, and that was scary. I tried to take care of Randy, but when Daddy came and took us to live with Grandma it was a big relief. It wasn't that I didn't love my

## Rejoicing in Hope

mother, but I didn't know how take care of Randy—I was only six years old—and sometimes we didn't have much to eat. That all changed when we moved in with Grandma."

Gary nodded. "I heard some of that from Mary, before I ever knew you. She was living with us when she went to look for her sister in Tucson. I only knew the bare outline, though."

Cecily sighed and snuggled up to Gary.

*****

Mary slowly recovered some of her strength, but the crisis left her sadly weakened. She was very thin, with a swollen, distended abdomen. She spent much of her day in bed and reluctantly turned over the last of her household responsibilities to Cecily and Randy.

On Christmas Day the weather was pleasant and Jason took Mary to the Ballard home for the festive dinner. He took soft foods and gelatin along for Mary, who was unable to tolerate the ordinary holiday menu. She now used a wheelchair whenever she went outside the home. Randy and Cecily brought little Jay to the Ballard's house in Cecily's car. He was excited and wriggled ecstatically in his car seat. Gary met them when they arrived at the Ballard home and helped Jay out. Then he extended his hand to Cecily.

"Your aunt and uncle are here, and the dinner is almost ready. The ham is done and Mom is fixing the gravy. All the other foods are ready to dish up, including the pies."

Cecily thanked him, and Randy playfully punched him in the arm. "Haven't you got cold feet yet, brother-in-law? Just a few more weeks and you'll be tethered and domesticated."

Gary punched him back and led them to the door of his home.

# Rejoicing in Hope

*****

Mary apparently enjoyed the holiday celebration, but she was so worn out from the exertion that she remained in bed the following days. Since this was Christmas vacation, Cecily was able to concentrate on making sure everything was ready for the wedding which would take place in a just over a week.

Randy devoted himself to the care of his little cousin in his free time, and noticed that little Jay was showing signs of anxiety about his mother. When Randy asked him what he was worrying about, he said, "Why is Mommy always sick? She never makes cookies for me any more, and she's always tired."

Randy paused, unsure of how to relieve his little cousin's anxiety. He didn't want to lie to him, naturally, and yet he wanted to avoid adding to Jay's worries.

"I don't know why your mommy is sick, but because she is sick she can't make cookies for you any more. I think, though, that you and I could make some cookies. Let's find a cook book and look up some easy recipes."

Jay's eyes lit up. "Yes, let's make some cookies. I like peanut butter cookies best."

Randy was in for it now. He had never made cookies, although he remembered "helping" his grandmother make some when he was small. He consulted Cecily, who found a recipe book that was especially designed for baking with children's help. So, while Cecily was busy with final preparations for her wedding, Randy was busy making a royal mess in the kitchen with Jay's help. When Cecily looked in on them, she was dismayed, but Randy assured her that "Jay and I will clean the place up. Not to worry."

# Rejoicing in Hope

# Rejoicing in Hope

## Chapter 35

On the morning of her wedding day Cecily was shocked to see that her Aunt Mary's skin had a pronounced yellowish cast. She was definitely jaundiced. Cecily's impressions were confirmed when her eyes sought out her uncle Jason. He nodded almost imperceptibly, but nothing was said. Mary decided to stay in bed all morning in order to conserve her strength for the wedding. Two hours before the wedding procession was scheduled to begin, Jean Ballard came to the Nealey house and helped Mary to get dressed for the event. She also applied makeup in an attempt to cover up the jaundice. While the makeup did improve her appearance, it could not entirely restore a normal skin color.

The sight of her aunt's face had shocked Cecily but she had no time to mull over this. Jason devoted himself to his wife who looked very ill, but who insisted on taking part in the procession, even though she had to enter in a wheelchair. Randy took little Jay under his wing. The little boy was frightened by his mother's appearance, and in a penetrating high-pitched voice, asked Randy: "What's wrong with Mommy? She looks so funny."

Randy shushed him and explained, "That's only because she's sick."

Secluded in one of the church's classrooms with her attendants, Cecily struggled with a lump in her throat. *Oh God, I always expected my wedding to be a deliriously happy time, but how can I be carefree when Aunt Mary is so sick!*

Paula Ballard dabbed the tears from Cecily's cheeks and helped her apply her makeup. "Don't cry, Cecily. Mary has looked forward to this day for a long time, and it means so much to her that she can see you married and launched on

# Rejoicing in Hope

your missionary career!" Paula herself was planning an early spring wedding to her beloved accountant.

Cecily nodded. She lifted her heart in prayer that God would give her strength to show Gary a happy face when she walked down the aisle. She was sure he didn't need a gloomy bride.

****

Years later Cecily would remember her wedding day as one of mingled grief and joy. She remembered walking down the aisle and looking into the eyes of her handsome, smiling bridegroom, waiting for her at the altar. After the ceremony she stopped to kiss her father, her Aunt Mary, and her Uncle Jason. She hugged Randy and Jay, and then proceeded back up the aisle to the vestibule, to finish the triumphant march. There the wedding party lined up to receive the congratulations and best wishes of the wedding guests.

But she also remembered glimpses of her Aunt Mary, now sadly altered from the sturdy, motherly person she knew. Her aunt was a mere shadow of her former self, leaning back in her wheelchair, smiling when addressed, and looking exhausted. Her husband never left her side.

She remembered seeing her stepmother at the wedding, but that was all. Susan did not come forward to congratulate the newlyweds.

Young Randy devoted himself to little Jay, who seemed to be having a wonderful time. Randy Senior approached the bridal party to chat with his daughter and son-in-law. He congratulated her on the very well-organized wedding and reception, saying that he would not have been able to manage as well on the budget he had granted her. She smiled and thanked him.

## Rejoicing in Hope

When the reception ended she excused herself to walk over to her aunt and uncle. She urged Jason to take his wife home, because she looked exhausted. He nodded, and left to move his car to the wheelchair-accessible exit of the building. Cecily stayed beside her aunt and said, "Aunt Mary, you look so tired. You were wonderful and have done so much for me, even in organizing my wedding. I think you should go home now and rest. I'll call you tomorrow."

Mary smiled wearily and acquiesced. Cecily stayed beside her aunt until her uncle brought his car up to the exit's ramp. She wheeled her aunt outside and helped her uncle to lift her into the car. Afterward she rejoined her bridegroom in the vestibule.

Gary took her hand in his, and smiled tenderly. "How are things going?"

"With Aunt Mary, you mean? Or with the reception?" Cecily tried to understand what he wanted to know.

"Neither. I mean with you. Are you all right?" He looked at her with concern.

"I'm fine. It's just that I'm worried about Aunt Mary. It's been too much for her, I think. She looks awful."

Gary nodded. "I know, but it's what she wanted more than anything. It would not have been right to cheat her of the satisfaction of seeing you married."

Cecily nodded. "True. She thinks the world of you and is delighted to have you in our family."

*****

After Cecily and Gary had changed into their travel clothes, they said goodbye to friends and family. Gary explained to them, "We'll stop in to see how Mary is doing tomorrow before heading out on our honeymoon. Thanks for everything."

# Rejoicing in Hope

Randy was carrying a sleeping Jay over his shoulder and hurried after his sister to ask for the keys to her car. She apologized, and handed them over to him. She gave him a sisterly kiss, and he turned to hunt up her Prizm in the parking lot.

As Gary opened the car door for her, Cecily became aware of a nervous thumping in her chest. She was about to pass through the mysterious door that separated the virgin from the wife, and she worried whether she would be adequate. Gary felt the change in her mood, and as they drove out of the parking lot, he turned to her.

"Feeling scared?" he asked.

"A little," she admitted.

"We're spending tonight in a hotel, and tomorrow we'll see Mary before we head out to Galveston. If you're not too tired, we could have devotions before we go to bed tonight."

"I'd like that," she said.

Suddenly there was no one else in the whole world except the man who was seated beside her. Her heart swelled with gratitude to God.

*****

The following morning they loaded their bags into Gary's car and drove to the Nealey house in Cedar Hill. Cecily found her uncle there, which she had not expected. He was rarely home during work hours because of the demands of his business. Cecily felt her anxiety rising.

"How is Aunt Mary?" Is she still in bed?"

Jason looked worried, but he answered her gently, "She had a bad night, and is resting in bed."

Cecily felt guilty of having brought her aunt too much stress. "It was too much for her, wasn't it?"

## Rejoicing in Hope

Jason smiled sadly. "Yes, it was, but it's what she wanted. She's been looking forward to the wedding for months. She felt this was something she could do for her sister Ingrid—your mother—you know. You made her very happy by giving her a role in your wedding."

Cecily swallowed the lump in her throat. "May I just slip into her room and see her?"

"Certainly." Jason led the way to the bedroom and quietly opened the door.

The room was shadowed, and as her eyes adjusted to the light she could discern her aunt's motionless form on the bed. She moved closer and bent over the inert figure lying there. She gently stroked the yellowed skin on her aunt's cheek.

Mary opened her eyes and smiled. Cecily squeezed her hand, and Mary responded by pressing hers affectionately. "Thanks for stopping by, Cecily. Are you on your way to your honeymoon now?" Her voice was only a whisper.

"Yes, yes we are, Aunt Mary. I'm sorry you're feeling so exhausted."

"That's all right. It was worth it. Now if I could only stop worrying about little Jay I would have perfect peace."

"Is there something I can do for him to relieve some of that worry, Aunt Mary?"

"Thanks, but I don't see how you can without taking him away from his Daddy. I wouldn't want that to happen. I'm praying for God to give me the grace I need to leave my dear ones—my husband and our little son—in his hands."

Cecily wept. She bent over the bed and prayed aloud: "Dear Lord, take us all into your hands and give Aunt Mary peace."

## Rejoicing in Hope

Then she kissed her aunt and turned to leave. She stumbled to the door, tears blinding her eyes. Her uncle stepped up to steady her and she threw her arms around him. She felt a firm yet gentle grip on her left arm, and she heard Gary say, "What's wrong, darling? Tell me."

She shook her head, unable to speak. Gary led her to the car. He made sure that her safety belt was buckled, and then asked, "Would you like to talk about it?"

Cecily shook her head. "It's just that she looks awful and is struggling with the knowledge that she has to leave her husband and son behind when she goes. I asked if I could help her with little Jay, but she said no; that would mean that he couldn't stay with his father. She doesn't want that to happen."

"I see." Gary realized that Cecily had offered to take in little Jay to assure he would be brought up in a loving home. But of course, if she was in Brazil that would mean that the little boy could not be with his father. He was unsure of what to say, so he put his arm around her and wiped her eyes with a tissue. Then he started the motor and they drove off to Galveston to begin their honeymoon.

# Rejoicing in Hope

## Chapter 36

The days following their wedding sped by as if on wings. After their honeymoon they returned to their previous responsibilities: Gary to his work in the Regional Office and Cecily to studying for her comprehensive exams.

Mary Nealy's health had improved enough that she could oversee some of the Nealey domestic affairs, but she could not longer participate in the Sunday dinner potlucks. Cecily and Gary joined the Ballard families (along with Carol and her husband) for the potluck meals, which now were held in the Ballard home. Jason, Randy, and Jay stayed home with Mary now because she found the potluck meal too strenuous.

Young Randy stayed in the Nealey house at his uncle's request, because of little Jay's attachment to him. He was now paying board and was making good progress in paying back his debts. He continued to work in his uncle's shipping business, but was taking an evening course and hoped to return to full time study when his debts should be paid in full.

One day little Jay was helping his cousin to put the supper dishes into the dishwasher and asked him, "Randy, why is Mommy always sick?"

Randy took a deep breath. *Lord, give me wisdom to answer his question simply and truthfully.* He put his arm around his little cousin.

"Your mother has a sickness called 'liver cancer,' and that's something that doesn't usually get better. But one day she'll go to live with Jesus and then she'll be completely well again. Jesus loves her so much that he wants her to come to live with him."

# Rejoicing in Hope

Jay blinked up at his cousin.

"Can I go to live with Jesus too when she goes? I want to go with her."

"Yes, Jesus wants you to live with him too, but probably not right away. Have you asked God to forgive your sins and give you a new heart? Without a new heart you can't live with Jesus."

Jay searched his cousin's face, trying to understand.

"If I ask Jesus for a new heart, will he let me go with Mommy?"

Randy swallowed a lump in his throat. "He probably won't take you right away. Just think how sad Daddy would be if both of you left!"

Jay nodded. He didn't want his Daddy to be sad and all alone, but he did want to go to Jesus and be with his Mommy. He tugged at Randy's sleeve, "Let's talk to Jesus and ask him for a new heart."

Randy was thrown off balance. He had never prayed with another person. He had never asked for a new heart for himself either, and he certainly needed it more than this worried little boy at his side, whom he had learned to love more than anyone else in the world.

"Okay." He knelt in the kitchen and Jay knelt beside him. "Dear Jesus, Jay and I need new hearts so that we can live with you. Please forgive us all the bad things we've done and teach us to be like you so that we can live with you some day. Amen."

They rose to their feet, and Jay said, "When is Mommy going to be with Jesus? Can she go right now?"

## Rejoicing in Hope

Randy's Bible background was skimpy indeed. He remembered something about Jesus "preparing a place" in his Father's house.[1]

"When he has a room ready for her, he'll call her."

"Oh," Jay replied, satisfied with the answer.

*****

Cecily took her comprehensive exams and passed them. Her father came to attend her graduation and stayed in his daughter's apartment. The tiny apartment had no guest room, so Randy Senior slept on the living room sofa. He had been shocked by how much Mary Nealey had changed in the few weeks since Cecily's wedding. He would not have known her. She was not only wasting away, but she was almost an orange color from jaundice. He noticed that his son had virtually taken over the care of his little cousin. This young man who showed so much concern for a little boy was not the same carefree, irresponsible youth he had bailed out of trouble only a few months ago.

When he was alone with his son, he asked him, "Have you decided to stay here and work instead of finishing your degree in Texarkana?"

"N-no," Randy replied slowly. "Not exactly. I'm taking evening courses here, and expect to transfer them back into my Texarkana program in another year or so."

His father eyed him thoughtfully. "What will determine when you'll move home and finish your course there?"

Randy looked up and met his father's eye. "I thought I'd like to get my debts paid up first, for one thing. For another, I think it would be hard on little Jay if I left right now. His

---

[1] John 14:2, 3

mother is dying, and he's going to need someone to help him over that."

"What about his father?" Where does he fit into this?"

Randy shrugged. "He's a great father, but he's kept pretty busy with his business and helping his wife through this. Cecily used to pitch in a lot before she got married, but she's been busy studying for her comps and hasn't been able to help out as much as she used to. Now that she's graduated, Gary will want her to meet some of the people who have pledged to support them overseas. She'll have her hands full, I think."

Randy Senior stood up and walked over to window. After a period of silence he turned and warned his son, "Just don't wait too long, son. Soon you'll want to start a family and then you'll be loaded down with responsibilities. It's easier to finish your studies while you're still single."

\*\*\*\*\*

In February Gary and Cecily met with the translation mission's director in charge of new members. He recommended a special reduction in the requirements for Cecily's survival training, taking into account her month's experience in Brazil and Gary's fulfillment of the requirements the year before. He suggested that both attend the first part of the training in Mexico, and then, with the approval of the Brazil Branch, that Cecily be supervised in a specially-designed tropical adaptation program in Brazil. This would allow them to go to their field assignment after only six weeks of the preliminary training. Gary was jubilant.

"I was afraid we wouldn't get to Brazil until the end of next year, but at this rate, we'll be able to go by the middle of the year. We're close to reaching our support quota goals now, so the end is in sight. Thank the Lord!"

# Rejoicing in Hope

Cecily's response was more reserved. She no longer worried about her brother, nor did she dread going to the more remote areas of Brazil since her visit to the Guará villages, but her Aunt Mary was failing rapidly and she hated to think about leaving her. She took the Mexican survival course that month, and Gary served on the teaching staff.

After Cecily's experience with the Guará in Brazil it was not much of a shock at all. Even the survival hikes and the camping in jungle hammocks were relatively uncomplicated experiences.

The course lasted six weeks. During this period she was able to keep abreast of her aunt's physical condition by corresponding with her brother. He reported that Mary's condition seemed to remain stable.

*****

When she returned from Mexico in March she found her aunt dozing in a recliner in the living room. She gently stroked her aunt's yellowed cheek, and Mary opened her eyes. Focusing on Cecily, she smiled.

"You're back! Glad to see you."

Cecily patted her aunt's wasted hand.

"I'm glad to be back. How are you?"

Mary squeezed her niece's hand in response. "I just had a wonderful dream. I dreamt that I saw Ingrid and told her about your wedding and your wonderful husband. She said she was very glad that everything was going well for you."

Cecily felt a lump in her throat. "Did you tell her I am going to Brazil with my wonderful husband?"

"I don't think so. I can't remember doing that." Mary wrinkled her forehead trying to remember.

# Rejoicing in Hope

Cecily spoke hesitantly. "When you see my Mom in heaven, can you tell her that I love her and that I hope to serve the Lord all my life, wherever he sends me?"

Mary smiled. "It's possible that she already knows. I look forward to seeing her there."

Cecily spoke with painful reluctance: "Aunt Mary, do you really think that my Mom is in heaven with Jesus? Is that possible, after wasting her whole life on drugs and promiscuity?"

Mary's eyes mirrored her love for the daughter of her wayward sister. "I find it easier to believe that the Lord forgave her at her last breath, than I do that he has forgiven me all the anger and bitterness I harbored during my youth. Even after I committed my life to him, I hung onto my resentment against my mother and sister. He has been so good to me, and I was so ungrateful."

"But Aunt Mary, surely you had a right to be angry. From what I heard, they were pretty mean to you."

"Maybe I had some right to resent that, but because I couldn't forgive them I took out my anger on some of the sweetest people in the world, like Rachel Kruyter. She's not the only one I wounded with my bitterness." Mary sighed, remembering the years in college, her rage at Miriam who took away her boyfriend, and irritation with colleagues like Beth Sanders in Brazil during the years in which she clung to her resentments.

Cecily was silent, trying to imagine the gentle, affectionate person lying in the recliner as someone seething with bitterness. "Then the Lord must have changed you, Aunt Mary, because I haven't seen anything like that in you during all the years I've known you."

## Rejoicing in Hope

Tears brimmed in Mary's eyes. "Yes, I know he did. And he filled my cup with joy during all the years since that furlough. That is what gives me hope."

*****

The following week Cecily began to accompany her husband on his trips to churches that had professed an interest in supporting them overseas. At first Cecily was shy when asked to tell about herself, but the audiences were on the whole warmly welcoming, and she soon felt more at ease with them. She did not altogether enjoy speaking at these meetings, but she soon lost much of her shyness.

When they returned to Dallas she learned that her Aunt Mary had been placed in hospice care because Jason was no longer able to give her all the care she required at home.

When Cecily walked into the hospice room she thought she must have mistaken the room number, because she did not recognize the wasted, copper-colored figure on the bed. She turned around and rechecked the name on the door. It was "Mary Nealey," without a doubt. She approached the bed and looked down at the woman lying there.

She touched her aunt's hand, but there was no response. She called gently, "Aunt Mary, Aunt Mary...," but there was not even a flicker of her eyelids.

Cecily turned blindly and walked out of the room. She almost walked into someone who was just entering. She wiped her eyes with the back of her hands and recognized her Uncle Jason, looking pale and worn. She hugged him.

"Aunt Mary isn't responding, is she?"

Jason shook his head. His voice was hoarse with emotion as he answered, "No, she's in a coma. She hasn't responded since yesterday. All her systems seem to be shutting down. She's going, Cecily!"

# Rejoicing in Hope

He took her arm and drew her to a deserted alcove designated for visitors, where coffee was available for their comfort. As they took their seats, Jason said, "She now seems beyond conflict, but she had a fierce spiritual struggle for several weeks."

Cecily stared. "She did?"

"Yes. She was overwhelmed with a sense of guilt for the years in which she had been unable to forgive the people who wronged her. Nothing I said seemed to comfort her. I even asked our pastor to bring her the assurance of God's forgiveness she needed, but his visit failed to comfort her.

"I sent an e-mail to Rachel, begging her to try to convince Mary that God's grace was sufficient for her. Rachel sent this message." Jason pulled some folded sheets out of an internal jacket pocket, and passed them over to Cecily. She read:

Dear Mary,

> Jason tells me you are troubled by all your shortcomings and sins, feeling unprepared to face your Maker. I want to remind you of something you already know, but seem to be losing sight of, now that the end of your pilgrimage is in sight.
>
> Nothing you have done, and nothing you could ever do, can qualify you for heaven. Even if you had been able to forgive those who wronged you years earlier, it would still not be enough. Only Christ's death on your behalf can qualify you for an eternity in heaven.
>
> There are two passages that I pray God will use to give you peace and the courage you need to face death.

## Rejoicing in Hope

"Therefore, since we have a great high priest who has gone through the heavens, Jesus the Son of God, let us hold firmly to the faith we profess. For we do not have a high priest who is unable to sympathize with our weaknesses, but we have one who has been tempted in every way, just as we are—yet was without sin. Let us then approach the throne of grace with confidence, so that we may receive mercy and find grace to help us in our time of need."[1]

The following passage seems to be directed especially to you:

"At one time we too were foolish, disobedient, deceived and enslaved by all kinds of passions and pleasures. We lived in malice and envy, being hated and hating one another. But when the kindness and love of God our Savior appeared, he saved us, not because of righteous things we had done, but because of his mercy. He saved us through the washing of rebirth and renewal by the Holy Spirit, whom he poured out on us generously through Jesus Christ our Savior, so that, having been justified by his grace, we might become heirs having the hope of eternal life. This is a trustworthy saying."[2]

Richard and I commend you to the One who loved you so much that he died for you.

Love in Jesus,

Rachel

---

[1] Hebrews 4:14-16
[2] Titus 3:3-8a

# Rejoicing in Hope

Jason explained, "I read this message to Mary, and she begged me to reread it several times. Then she took the sheet into her hands and closed her eyes. Later that day she asked me to read the passages over and over again. Finally she said, "I know the verses now, and I know that his grace is enough for me."

Cecily wept, remembering the conversation she had had with her aunt some months ago when she had questioned whether her own mother's "last breath" turning to Jesus was a real conversion.

As they walked back to Mary's room, Cecily asked, "Has little Jay been able to say goodbye to her?"

"Yes, I brought him here just two days ago so he could say goodbye. She knew him and smiled at him, but he was badly shaken up. I still wonder if I did the right thing."

Cecily nodded. "I know." *He probably couldn't recognize her: she has changed so much.*

She slipped her hand in her uncle's and together they faced their unconscious loved one. Cecily prayed silently, *Take her in your arms gently, Lord. Take her gently.*

# Rejoicing in Hope

## Chapter 37

August found Cecily shivering in the tiny unheated Brazilian apartment. It was winter in the southern hemisphere, and the cold penetrated through her sweater. She was sitting near a large picture window with a textbook entitled *Portuguese for Foreigners,* subtitled *Português para Estrangeiros* lying open before her. Across the room from her Gary was also studying from the same language text. She looked out at the urban scene before her. They were in Campinas, São Paulo, attending a language school that trained foreign missionaries for Christian work in Brazil.

Her computer monitor signaled that she had "mail." She leaned over and saw that it was a message from Rachel Kruyter. She downloaded the e-mail message that had just come through from the translator working with the Guará Indians in Minas Gerais State:

> Dear Cecily and Gary,
>
> It's nice to know that you're finally in Brazil with us, although you don't really seem any closer, because we still have to communicate by e-mail.
>
> People like Gary and you encourage us to hope for the future. The easily accessible people groups have been reached and now you young people are reaching out to the more difficult-to-reach groups. May God bless you and grant you the courage you will need to carry out his mandate. What a privilege is yours to tell the good news to people who have never heard!

# Rejoicing in Hope

Our work has its funny side as well as the serious. This morning a committee of Guará women visited me. There were three of them, and they entered our house giggling. I wondered what was so funny, but after they left, I felt a little inclined to giggle, too. Little Maria, a chatty lady, was the spokeswoman.

"Your child is getting big. Do you have another baby inside your belly?"

I was taken aback, and wasn't sure I was hearing correctly. "What did you say?"

She repeated her message: "Your child is big. Do you have another in your belly?" Then she explained, "When your child is big, you must get another inside your belly."

In our society this kind of question would be considered a rude intrusion into a woman's privacy, but there is no such privacy here. I stuttered to assure them that I had no "baby inside."

The Guará believe that a woman ought to have a child every two years. The infant mortality rate is high; therefore many babies must be produced to keep the population up.

As far as translation is concerned, Richard is working on Galatians, which is a challenging book. For example, we have a list of "fruit of the Spirit," and "acts of the sinful nature."[1] Finding native expressions for all of these terms is no small task.

---

[1] Galatians 5:19-23

# Rejoicing in Hope

Richard and I sat down and tried to differentiate "envy," "jealousy," and "covetousness." We decided that *envy* is resenting someone because they have something we don't have. *Jealousy* is when someone has something that we are sure ought to be ours. *Covetousness* is when we simply want something someone else has.

But even after we decide on the subtle meaning differences we still need to search for the native words that come close to those meanings.

We had quite a time looking for those terms. We found out that *xup kumĩy* means *envy*, and *putup* (want) will probably do for *covet*, but we hadn't found a word for *jealousy*.

One day Joana came over and brought her three-year-old granddaughter along. She put her down and picked up our Hannah and took her in her lap. The granddaughter began to fuss and tug at Hannah as if to pull her off her grandmother's lap. Joana smiled at me, and explained, "*Tute yĩp kumĩy*)." She handed Hannah back to me and took her little granddaughter back on her lap, who subsided contentedly.

That is how we learned that the term for *jealousy* is *yĩp kumĩy*. The little girl didn't like seeing someone else in the lap she believed she had a right to.

Love,

# Rejoicing in Hope

Rachel, for Richard, Laura Marie, Jerry, and Hannah.

Cecily called Gary to come over and read Rachel's message. As she did so, she remembered Rachel's words that "nothing binds a couple together like shared values and goals."

*****

Cecily turned back to the Portuguese textbook but soon allowed her mind to wander. She remembered seeing her dying aunt—now unrecognizable—in the hospice. If it had not been for the name plate on the door, she would not have believed that it could be her aunt lying motionless in the bed.

In her heart she said goodbye to her that day, and drove to her uncle's shipping office. A long-time employee was sitting at her uncle's desk and was taking an order on the telephone, so she turned and went to the store room. She found her brother working there, and gave him a hug.

"I'm back, Randy. How are you doing?"

Randy's face lit up, but then resumed the grave expression it had worn when she entered.

"Have you seen Aunt Mary yet?" he said.

"Yes, I did. I wouldn't have known her."

Randy nodded. "She's almost bronze-colored from jaundice and sleeps most of the time."

"She didn't wake up when I touched her and called her name. I think she's in a coma now."

"Probably," Randy agreed. "Have you seen little Jay yet?"

Cecily shook her head. "No, I haven't. Where is he?"

## Rejoicing in Hope

"He stays with the Matthews family during the day. They have kids Jay's age and he needs some playmates. Uncle Jason stays with Aunt Mary most of the time now, so I take Jay to school after breakfast and Jane Matthews picks him up after school. I bring him home after work and fix him his supper. He still sleeps at home, but that's about all."

"Are you still living there?" Cecily knew he had planned to move into his own apartment several weeks earlier.

"Yes, Uncle Jason asked me to stay on account of Jay. It's rough on the little guy. He tries so hard to understand it, but he can't."

"Has anyone told him what he can expect, that his mother is dying, I mean?"

"I told him that his mother is going to heaven to be with Jesus. I told him that a month or so ago, but of course, he doesn't know what to expect. He used to ask why he couldn't go with her, but he doesn't any more."

"I saw Uncle Jason at the hospice."

Randy sighed. "He's taking it pretty hard. She's the love of his life you know, ever since junior high. He told me that once."

Cecily stared at him. "I never knew that. Do you mean that she didn't reciprocate until after she'd been on the mission field for almost ten years?"

"I guess not." Randy picked up a carton to stack it in its appropriate place, and Cecily left the store room.

*****

Cecily's thoughts were brought back to the day of Mary's funeral which had been held in the church. Only three months earlier Gary and Cecily had been married in that same church, and Mary Nealey had been important in

## Rejoicing in Hope

planning that event. Now she lay in a casket in the vestibule of the church, while many people who had been blessed by her life and ministry lined up to "view the remains." As a result of the undertaker's art, she looked very much the way Cecily remembered her from earlier days.

As she stood near the bier to greet Jason and Mary's friends, she could not help contrasting this funeral with that of the little six-year-old Guará girl she had seen, who was buried "as is," without any cosmetic treatment of her corpse.

While the majority of the "viewers" were middle-aged, there were a significant number of Mary's former students who came to pay their last respects to a loved teacher. Several of them knew Gary and Cecily and paused to share unique ways in which Mary had blessed their lives.

One middle-aged woman lingered over the casket a long time. She was a stranger to Cecily. She looked up and saw that Cecily was watching her, so she walked over to her.

"You're not Mary White's daughter, are you?" she asked.

Cecily seized on the visitor's use of Mary's maiden name.

"No, I'm Cecily Ballard, her niece. She doesn't have a daughter. Did you know her before she was married?"

"Yes," she said. Then she saw that Cecily was still waiting for an explanation. "I'm Beth Walker; I was her partner in Brazil for seven years. We split up when I got married."

Cecily realized that this woman was someone who had known her aunt very well during the years when she was seething with bitterness.

"My aunt didn't talk very much about those years, but when she was dying she grieved over them. She had what

# Rejoicing in Hope

they call a 'bruised background.' I didn't get to know her until I was thirteen years old, after my mother died, but she was a very loving person and I thank God every day for her."

Mrs. Walker's face softened. "I'm so glad. She was very lonely and unhappy when I knew her. How wonderful that God turned her life around and gave her joy!"

*****

As Cecily recalled this conversation, her heart swelled in thanksgiving. She knelt beside her chair and prayed, *Lord, you've blessed me in so many ways. You brought Grandma Spears into my life when I was little and so scared. You brought Aunt Mary to tell me my mother died, and gave me hope that her life had come to a good end. You used Aunt Mary and Uncle Jason to lead me to know you and to teach me to pray. You brought Gary and his love into my life, and you took my brother Randy into your hands and turned him around. You gave Aunt Mary peace in her final hours. What a privilege to bring this message of hope to people who have never heard it in a language they can understand!"*

Gary looked up from his textbook and noticed that his wife was kneeling and wiping her eyes with a tissue. He arose and walked over to her.

"What's wrong, sweetheart? Why are you crying?"

"Mostly because I'm so thankful for all God has done for me and for those I love. How wonderful to have the hope of eternal life!"[1]

Gary knelt beside her, put his arms around her and prayed aloud, "Thank you, Lord, for so many blessings we can't even count them. Most of all, thanks for sending Jesus to die for us and for pouring out your love into our hearts,

---

[1] Romans 5:2

## Rejoicing in Hope

giving us the hope of eternal life. Now help us to pass on this message of hope to people who have never heard it."